Savages

Don Winslow

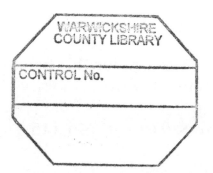

W F HOWES LTD

This large print edition published in 2010 by
W F Howes Ltd
Unit 4, Rearsby Business Park, Gaddesby Lane,
Rearsby, Leicester LE7 4YH

1 3 5 7 9 10 8 6 4 2

First published in the United Kingdom in 2010
by William Heinemann

A CIP catalogue record for this book is available
from the British Library

ISBN 978 1 40746 115 1

Typeset by Palimpsest Book Production Limited,
Falkirk, Stirlingshire
Printed and bound in Great Britain
by MPG Books Ltd, Bodmin, Cornwall

FSC
Mixed Sources
Product group from well-managed
forests, controlled sources and
recycled wood or fiber
SA-COC-1565
www.fsc.org
© 1996 Forest Stewardship Council

To Thom Walla.
On or off the ice.

'Going back to California,
So many good things around.
Don't want to leave California,
The sun seems to never go down.'

—JOHN MAYALL, 'CALIFORNIA'

1

Fuck you.

2

Pretty much Chon's attitude these days.

Ophelia says that Chon doesn't have attitude, he has 'baditude.'

'It's part of his charm,' O says.

Chon responds that it's a *muy* messed-up daddy who names his daughter after some crazy chick who drowns herself. That is some very twisted wish fulfillment.

It wasn't her dad, O informs him, it was her mom. Chuck was 404 when she was born, so Paqu had it her own way and tagged the baby girl 'Ophelia.' O's mother, Paqu, isn't Indian or anything, 'Paqu' is just what O calls her.

'It's an acronym,' she explains.

P.A.Q.U.

Passive Aggressive Queen of the Universe.

'Did your mother hate you?' Chon asked her this one time.

'She didn't hate me,' O answered. 'She hated *having* me because she got all fat and stuff – which for Paqu was five LBs. She popped me and bought a treadmill on the way home from the hospital.'

Yah, yah, yah, because Paqu is totally SOC R&B. South Orange County Rich and Beautiful.

Blonde hair, blue eyes, chiseled nose, and BRMCB – Best Rack Money Can Buy (you have real boobs in the 949 you're, like, Amish) – the extra Lincoln wasn't going to sit well or long on *her* hips. Paqu got back to the three-million-dollar shack on Emerald Bay, strapped little Ophelia into one of those baby packs, and hit the treadmill.

Walked two thousand miles and went nowhere.

'The symbolism is cutting, no?' O asked when wrapping the story up. She figures it's where she got her taste for machinery. 'Like, it had to be this powerful subliminal influence, right? I mean I'm this baby and there's this steady rhythmic humming sound and buzzers and flashing lights and shit? Come *on.*'

Soon as she was old enough to know that Ophelia was Hamlet's bipolar little squeeze with borderline issues who went for a one-way swim, she insisted that her friends start calling her just 'O.' They were cooperative, but there are some risks to glossing yourself 'O,' especially when you have a rep for glass-shattering climaxes. She was upstairs at a party one time with this guy? And

2

she started singing her happy song? And they could hear her downstairs over the music and everything. The techno was pounding but O was coming in like five octaves on top of it. Her friends laughed. They'd been to sleepovers when O had busted out the industrial-strength lots-o-moving-parts rabbit, so they knew the chorus.

'Is it live?' her bud Ashley asked. 'Or is it Memorex?'

O wasn't embarrassed or anything. Came back downstairs all loose and happy and shit, shrugged, 'What can I say? I like coming.'

So her friends know her as 'O,' but her girls tag her 'Multiple O.' Could have been worse, could have been 'Big O,' except she's such a small girl. Five five and skinny. Not bulimic or anorexic like three-quarters of the chicks in Laguna, she just has a metabolism like a jet engine. Burns fuel like crazy. This girl can eat and this girl doesn't like to throw up.

'I'm pixielike,' she'll tell you. 'Gamine.'

Yeah, not quite.

This gamine has Technicolor tatts down her left arm from her neck to her shoulder – silver dolphins dancing in the water with golden sea nymphs, big blue breaking waves, bright green underwater vines twisting around it all. Her formerly blonde hair is now blonde and *blue* with vermilion streaks and she has a stud in her right nostril. Which is to say—

Fuck you, Paqu.

Beautiful day in Laguna.

Aren't they all, though?

What Chon thinks as he looks out at another sunny day. One after the other after the other after the—

Other.

He thinks about Sartre.

Ben's condo is plunked on a bluff that juts out over Table Rock Beach, and a prettier place you've never seen, which it better be given the zeros that Ben plunked down for it. Table Rock is a big boulder that sits about fifty yards – depending on the tide – into the ocean and resembles, okay, a table. You don't have to be a Mensa member to figure that out.

The living room in which he sits is all floor-to-ceiling tinted windows so you can drink in every drop of the gorgeous view – oceans and cliffs and Catalina on the horizon – but Chon's eyes are glued to the laptop screen.

O walks in, looks at him, and asks, 'Internet porn?'

'I'm addicted.'

'Everyone's addicted to Internet porn,' she says. Including herself – she likes it a lot. Likes to log on, type in 'squirters,' and check out the clips. 'It's cliché for a guy. Can't you be addicted to something else?'

'Like?'

'I dunno,' she answers. 'Heroin. Go for the retro thing.'

'HIV?'

'You could get clean needles.' She thinks it might be cool to have a junkie lover. When you're done fucking him and don't want to deal with him you just prop him on the floor in the corner. And there's the whole tragically hip thing. Until that got boring and then she could do the intervention drama and then go visit him at rehab on weekends and when he got out they could go to meetings together. Be all serious and spiritual and shit until *that* got boring. Then do something else.

Mountain biking, maybe.

Anyway, Chon's thin enough to be a junkie, all tall, angular, muscled – looks like something put together from junkyard metal. Sharp edges. Her friend Ash says you could cut yourself fucking Chon, and the cunt probably knows.

'I texted you,' O says.

'I didn't check.'

He's still eyeing the screen. Must be hot hot hot, she thinks. About twenty seconds later he asks, 'What did you text?'

'That I was coming over.'

'Oh.'

She doesn't even remember when John became Chon and she's known him practically all his life, since like preschool. He had baditude even then. Teachers hated Chon. *Ha-a-a-a-ated* him. He dropped out two months before high school graduation. It's not that Chon is stupid – he's off-the-charts smart; it's just his baditude.

O reaches for the bong on the glass coffee table. 'Mind if I smoke up?'

'Step lightly,' he warns her.

'Yeah?'

He shrugs. 'It's *your* afternoon.'

She grabs the Zippo and lights up. Takes a moderate hit, feels the smoke go into her lungs, spread across her belly, then fill her head. Chonny wasn't lying – it is *powerful* hydro – as one would expect from Ben & Chonny's, who produce the best hydro this side of . . .

Nowhere.

They just produce the best hydro, period.

O is instantly wreck-ed.

Lies faceup on the sofa and lets the high wash over and through her. *Amaaaaazing* dope, amazing grace, it makes her skin tingle. Gets her horny. Big wow, *air* gets O horny. She unsnaps her jeans, slides her fingers down, and starts strumming her tune.

Classic Chon, O thinks – although she's almost beyond thought, what with the super-dope and her bud blossoming – he'd rather sit there and stare at pixilated sex than boff a real woman lying within arm's reach, humping her hand.

'Come do me,' she hears herself say.

Chon gets up from his chair, slowly, like it's a chore. Stands over her and watches for a few seconds. O would grab him and pull him down

6

but one hand is busy (buzzy?) and it seems like too far a reach. *Finally* he unzips and yeah, she thinks, you too-cool-for-school, detached zen master Ash fucker, you're diamond hard.

He starts off all cool and controlled, deliberate like his dick is a pool cue and he's lining up his shots, but after a while he starts angerfucking her, *bam bam bam*, like he's shooting her. Drives her small shoulders into the arm of the sofa.

Trying to fuck the war out of himself, hips thrusting like he can fuck the images off, like the bad pictures will come out with his jizz (wargasm?), but it won't happen it won't happen it won't happen it won't happen even though she does her part arches her own hips and bucks like she's trying to throw him out of the fern grotto this machine invader cutting down her rain forest her slick moist jungle.

As she goes—
Oh, oh, oh.
Oh, oh, *ohhhhh* . . .
O!

4

When she wakes up—
—sort of—
Chon is sitting at the dining room table, still staring at the lappie, but now he's cleaning a gun broken down into intricate pieces on a beach

towel. Because Ben would fucking *freak* if Chon got oil on the table or the carpet. Ben is fussy about his things. Chon says he's like a woman but Ben has a different take. Each nice thing represents a risk – growing and moving hydro.

Even though Ben hasn't been here in months, Chon and O are still careful with his stuff.

O hopes the gun parts don't mean Chon's getting ready to go back to I-Rock-and-Roll, as he calls it. He's been back twice since getting out of the military, on the payroll of one of those sketchy private security companies. Returns with, as he says, his soul empty and his bank account full.

Which is why he goes in the first place.

You sell the skills you have.

Chon got his GED, joined the navy, and busted his way into SEAL school. Sixty miles south of here, on Silver Strand, they used the ocean to torture him. Made him lie faceup in a winter sea as freezing waves pounded him (waterboarding was just part of the drill, my friends, SOP). Put heavy logs on his shoulder and made him run up sand dunes and thigh-deep in the ocean. Had him dive underwater and hold his breath until he thought his lungs would blow his insides out. Did everything they could think of to make him ring the bell and quit – what they didn't get was that Chon *liked* the pain. When they finally woke up to that twisted fact, they taught him to do everything that a seriously crazy, crazily athletic man could do in H_2O.

8

Then they sent him to Stanland.

Afghanistan.

Where . . .

You got sand, you got snow, you ain't got no ocean.

The Taliban don't surf.

Neither does Chon, he hates that faux-cool shit, he always liked being the one straight guy in Laguna who *didn't* surf, he just found it funny that they spent six figures training him to be Aquaman and then shipped him to a place where there's no water.

Oh well, you take your wars where you can find them.

Chon stayed in for two enlistments and then checked out. Came back to Laguna to . . .

To . . .

Uhnnn . . .

To . . .

Nothing.

There was nothing for Chon *to* do. Nothing he wanted, anyway. He could have gone the lifeguard route, but he didn't feel like sitting on a high chair watching tourists work on their melanoma. A retired navy captain gave him a gig selling yachts but Chon couldn't sell and hated boats, so that didn't work out. So when the corporate recruiter looked him up, Chon was available.

To go to I-Rock-and-Roll.

Nasty *nasty* shit in those pre-Surge days, what with kidnappings, beheadings, IEDs severing sticks and blowing off melons. It was Chon's job to keep any of that shit from happening to the paying customers, and if the best defense is a good offense, well . . .

It was what it was.

And with the right blend of hydro, speed, Vike, and Oxy it was actually a pretty cool video game – IraqBox – and you could rack up some serious points in the middle of the Shia/Sunni/AQ-in-Mesopotamia cluster-fuck if you weren't too particular about the particulars.

O has diagnosed Chon with PTLOSD.

Post-Traumatic Lack Of Stress Disorder. He says he has no nightmares, nerves, flashbacks, hallucinations, or guilt.

'I wasn't stressed,' Chon insisted, 'and there was no trauma.'

'Must have been the dope,' O opined.

Dope is good, Chon agreed.

Dope is supposed to be bad, but in a *bad world* it's *good,* if you catch the reverse moral polarity of it. Chon refers to drugs as a 'rational response to insanity,' and his chronic use of the chronic is a chronic response to *chronic* insanity.

It creates balance, Chon believes. In a fucked-up world, you have to be fucked up, or you'll fall . . .

off . . .

the . . .

end—

5

O pulls her jeans up, walks over to the table, and looks at the gun, still in pieces on the beach towel. The metal parts are pretty in their engineered precision.

As previously noted, O likes power tools.

Except when Chon is cleaning one with professional concentration even though he's looking at a computer screen.

She looks over his shoulder to see what's so good.

Expects to see someone giving head, someone getting it, because there is no give without the get, no get without the give when it comes to head.

Not so fast.

Because what she sees is this clip:

A camera slowly pans across what looks like the interior of a warehouse at a line of nine severed heads set on the floor. The faces – all male, all with unkempt black hair – bear expressions of shock, sorrow, grief, and even resignation. Then the camera tilts up to the wall, where the trunks of the decapitated bodies hang neatly from hooks, as if the heads had placed them in a locker room before going to work.

There is no sound on the clip, no narration, just the faint sound of the camera and whoever is wielding it.

For some reason, the silence is as brutal as the images.

O fights back the vomit she feels bubbling up in her belly. Again, as previously noted, this is not a girl who likes to yank. When she gets some air back, she looks at the gun, looks at the screen, and asks, 'Are you going back to Iraq?'

Chon shakes his head.

No, he tells her, not Iraq. San Diego.

6

OMG.
RU Reddy 4—
Decapitation porn?
Check that.
Gay decapitation porn?!

O knows that Chon is seriously twisted – no, she *knows* Chon is seriously twisted – but not like day-old-spaghetti-in-a-bowl twisted, like getting off on guys getting their heads lopped off, like that TV show about the British king, every cute chick he fucks ends up getting her head cut off. (Moral of television show: if you give a guy really good head (heh heh), he thinks you're a whore and breaks up with you. Or: Sex = Death.)

'Who *sent* this to you?' O asks him.

Is it viral, floating around on YouTube, the MustSee vid-clip of the day? MySpace, Facebook (no, that isn't funny), Hulu? Is this what everyone's watching today, forwarding to their friends, you gotta check this out?

'Who sent this to you?' she repeats.

'Savages,' Chon says.

7

Chon doesn't say much.

People who don't know him think this is because he lacks vocabulary. The opposite is true – Chon doesn't use a lot of words because he likes them *so* much. Values them, so he tends to keep them for himself.

'It's like people who like quarters,' O explained one time. 'People who *like* quarters hate to *spend* quarters. So they always *have* a lot of quarters.'

Okay, she was *ripped* at the time.

But not wrong.

Chon always has a lot of words in his head, he just doesn't let them out of his mouth very often.

Take 'savage.'

Singular of 'savages.'

Chon is intrigued by the noun versus the adjective of it, the chicken and the egg, the cause and effect of that particular etymology. This conundrum (*nice* fucking word) emerged from a conversation he overheard in Stanland. The topic was Fundolslamos who threw acid in little girls' faces for the sin of going to school.

Here's the scene that Chon remembers:

EXT. SEAL TEAM FIREBASE – DAY

A group of SEALS – worn out from the firefight – stand around a coffee urn set on a mess table.

SEAL TEAM MEDIC
(shocked, appalled)
How can you account for people doing some-thing so . . . savage?

SEAL TEAM LEADER
(jaded)
Easy – they're savages.

CUT TO:

8

Chon gets what the clip is: Video Conferencing. In which the Baja Cartel makes the following deal points:

1. You will not sell your hydro retail.
2. *We* will sell your hydro retail.
3. You will sell *us* your hydro wholesale, and at a price.
4. Or—
    —let's go to the videotape.

In this illustrative visual aid (an educational tool) we see five former drug merchants, formerly of the Tijuana/San Diego Metroplex, who insisted on representing the retail version of their product in contravention of our previously stated demands, and four former Mexican police officers, formerly of Tijuana, who provided them protection (or not, as the case may be).

These guys were all fucking idiots.

We think you're much smarter.

Watch and learn.

Don't make us go live.

9

Chon explains this to O.

The Baja Cartel, with its corporate headquarters in Tijuana, exports by land, sea, and air a shitload of boo, coke, smack, and meth into the USofA. Originally they just controlled the crossborder smuggling itself and left the retail end to others. In recent years, however, they have moved to vertically integrate all ends of the trade, from production and transportation to marketing and sales.

They accomplished this with relative ease in regard to heroin and cocaine, but had to overcome some early resistance from American motorcycle gangs that controlled the methamphetamine trade.

The biker gangs quickly grew tired of throwing lavish funerals (have you checked the price of beer lately?) and agreed to join the BC sales team, and ER doctors across America were pleased that meth production became standardized so they would know what biochemical symptoms to expect when the ODs came rolling in.

However, sales figures for the three afore-mentioned drugs have sharply declined. There is a relentless Darwinian factor in meth use particularly, in which its users die off or become brain-dead so quickly they can't figure out where to buy the product. (If you think you hate junkies, you haven't met tweekers. Tweekers make junkies look like John Wooden.) And although heroin seems to be making a tenuous but noticeable recovery, the BC still needs to replace the declining income to keep its shareholders happy.

So now it wants to control the entire marijuana market and eliminate competition from the mom-and-pop hydro growers in SoCal.

'Like Ben and Chonny's,' O says.

Chon nods.

The cartel will let them stay in business only if they sell solely *to* the cartel, which will then take the big profit margin for itself.

'They're Walmart,' O says.

(Have we covered that O is not stupid?)

They *are* Walmart, Chon agrees, and they have moved horizontally to offer a wide variety of products – they sell not only drugs, but human beings for both the labor and sex markets, and they have recently entered into the lucrative kidnapping business.

But that is not relevant to this discussion or the vid-clip in question, which graphically illustrates that—

Ben and Chonny can take

De Deal
Or
De Capitation.

10

'Are you going to take the deal?' O asks. Chon snorts, 'No.'

He turns off the laptop and starts reassembling the pretty gun.

11

O goes home.

Where Paqu is in one of her phases.

O has a hard time keeping up with her phases –
But in rough order:

Yoga
Pills and alcohol
Rehab
Republican politics
Jesus
Republican politics and Jesus
Fitness
Fitness, Republican politics, and Jesus
Cosmetic surgery
Gourmet cooking
Jazzercise
Buddhism
Real estate

Real estate, Jesus, and Republican politics
Fine wine
Re-rehab
Tennis
Horseback riding
Meditation

And now—

Direct sales.

'It's a pyramid scheme, Mom,' O said when she saw the boxes and boxes of organic skin-care products that Paqu tried to enlist her to sell. She'd already signed up most of her friends, who were all selling the shit to one another in a sort of merchandizing circle-jill.

'It's not a pyramid scheme,' Paqu objected. 'A pyramid scheme is like those cleaning products.'

'And this—'

'Isn't,' Paqu said.

'Have you ever seen a pyramid?' O asked her. 'Or a picture of one?'

'Yes.'

'Okay,' O said, wondering why she was even trying. 'You sell this crap and kick up a percentage to the person who enlisted you. You enlist other people who kick up to you. That's a pyramid, Mom.'

'No, it isn't.'

O gets home this afternoon and Paqu is on the

patio slamming *mojitos* with all her Organic Makeup Cult buddies. They're all buzzed and buzzing about some upcoming motivational three-day cruise event.

Which would make you root for Somali pirates, O thinks.

'Can I fix you some Kool-Aid?' O asks the women graciously.

Paqu is oblivious. 'Thank you, dear, but we have refreshments. Wouldn't you like to join us?'

Yes I wouldn't, O thinks.

'I'm otherwise engaged,' she says, retreating to the relative sanctuary of her room.

Six is hiding in his home office pretending to be tracking the market but really watching an Angels game. The door is open and he sees O and quickly swivels around to peer into his computer monitor.

'Don't worry,' O says. 'I won't squeal.'

'You want a martini?'

'I'm good.'

She goes into her room, flops on the bed, and crashes.

12

Lado is short for 'Helado,' which is Spanish for 'stone cold.'

It fits.

Miguel Arroyo, aka Lado, is stone cold.

(A figure of speech that Chon would object to,

BTW. Having been to the desert, he knows that stones can be fucking hot.)

Anyway—

Even as a kid, Lado didn't seem to have any feelings, or if he did, he didn't show them anyway. Hug him – his mother did, a lot – you got nothing. Whip his ass with a belt – his father did, a lot – the same nothing. He'd just look at you with those black eyes, like what do you want with me?

He's no kid now. Forty-six, he's a father himself. Two sons and a teenage daughter who is making him *loco*. Of course, that's her job at her age. No kid, he has himself a wife, a nice landscaping business, he makes money. No one takes a belt to him anymore.

Now he drives his Lexus through San Juan Capistrano, looking at the nice *futbol* field, then turns left into the big housing community, block after block of identical apartment buildings behind a stone wall that runs alongside the railroad track.

NBM.

Nothing But Mexicans.

Block after block.

You hear English here it's the mailman talking to himself.

This is where the nice Mexicans live. Where the respectful, respectable, hardworking Mexicans live when they're not at their jobs. These are old Mexican families, been here since before the Anglos stole it, were here when the Spanish fathers

20

came to steal it first. Put the stones in the mission for the swallows to come back to.

These are Mexican-Americans, send their kids to the nice Catholic school across the street, where the faggot priests will train them to be docile. These are the nice Mexicans who dress up on Sundays and after mass go to the park or down to the grassy strips along the harbor in Dana Point and have cookouts. Sunday is Mexicans' Day Out, pray to Jesus and pass the tortillas *por favor*.

Lado is not a nice Mexican.

He's one of those scary Mexicans.

A former Baja State cop, he has big hands with broken knuckles, scars from blades and bullets. Black black obsidian eyes. He's seen that Mel Gibson movie about Mexico back in the Majan days when they ripped people's bellies open with obsidian blades and his *viejos* say that he has eyes like those knives.

Back in the day Lado was one of Los Zetas, the special counternarcotics task force in Baja. He survived the narco wars of the nineties, saw a lot of men killed, more than a few at his own hands, busted a lot of the narcos himself, took them into alleys and made them give up their secrets.

He laughs at the news reports about 'torture' in Iraq and Afghanistan. They were using waterboarding in Mexico since before Lado can remember, except they didn't use water but

Coca-Cola – the carbonation gave it a little more zing and motivated your narco to bubble up with useful information.

Now the U.S. Congress is going to investigate.

Investigate what?

The *world?*

Life?

What goes on between men?

How else do you make a bad man tell you the truth? You think you smile at him, give him sandwiches and cigarettes, become his friend? He'll smile back and lie to you and think what a *cabrón* you are.

But that was back in the old days, before he and the rest of the Zetas got tired of busting drugs and making no money, of working their asses off and dying while they watched the narcos get rich, before they decided to get rich themselves.

Lado's eyes are cold stone?

Maybe because those eyes have seen—

His own hands holding a chain saw

Swooping through a man's neck as

Blood sprayed.

Your eyes would be hard, too.

Your eyes would turn to stone.

Some of those seven men they begged, they cried, they pleaded to God, to their mamas, they said they had families, they pissed their trousers. Others said nothing, just looked with the silent resignation that Lado thinks is the expression of

22

Mexico itself. Bad things are going to happen, it is simply a matter of when. They should stitch that on the flag.

He's glad to be El Norte.

He goes now to find this kid Esteban.

13

Esteban lives in the big housing project and has an inquiring attitude.

Questions for the Anglo world.

You want me to get a job? Mow your lawn? Clean your pool, flip your burgers, make your tacos? This is what we came here for? Paid the coyotes? Crawled under the fence, trudged across the desert?

You want me to be one of those good Mexicans, one of those hardworking, churchgoing, family-valuing, get dressed in my best clothes on Sunday and walk with my cousins down those broad sun-baked boulevards to a park named after Chavez, humble respectful nigger taco Mexicans, the ones we all love and respect and pay subminimum wage?

Like my *papi*?

Out in his pickup before the sun, the truck with the rakes sticking out, trimming the *gueros'* lawns so they look so green and pretty. Comes home at night so *chingada* tired he don't want to talk, he don't want to do nothing except eat, drink a beer, go to sleep. Does this six days a week, stops only on Sunday to be a humble respectful nigger taco Mexican to God, give the money he sweats for to God and the faggot priests. Sunday is his *papi*'s big day, the day he puts on a clean white shirt, clean white pants (no grass stains on the knees), shoes that come out once a week, wiped off with a clean cloth, and he takes his family to church and after church they get together with all the aunts and aunties, the *tios* and *tias*, with all the cousins, and they go to the park and cook *came* and *pollo* and smile at their pretty daughters in their pretty little Sunday dresses and it is so *chingada* boring that Esteban would lose it if he hadn't snuck off after church for a hit, drawn the sweet smoke in, chilled himself out.

Like mi madre? Works in the hotels, cleans the *gueros'* toilets, scrubs their shit and puke out of the bowls? Always on her knees, if not on bathroom tiles, then on church pews. A devout woman, she always smells like disinfectant.

Esteban had a job for a while at one of Machado's taco stands. Worked his ass off chopping onions, washing dishes, taking out the garbage, and for what? Pocket change. Then his *papi* got him hired on to one of Mr Arroyo's landscaping crews. Better money, but backbreaking, boring work.

But Esteban he needs money.

Lourdes is pregnant.

How did that happen?

Of course he knows how it happened. Saw her

24

on a Sunday afternoon in one of those pretty white dresses. Her black eyes and long black lashes, the breasts under that dress. Went up and talked to her, smiled at her, walked over to the grill and brought her back something to eat. Talked nice to her, made nice talk with her mother, her father, her cousins, her aunts.

She was one of those good girls, a virgin, maybe that's what attracted him, she wasn't one of the gangbanger sluts who will go to her knees for anyone.

He called on her for three months, three months before the family would let them be alone, and then three more months of hot, torturous afternoons of visiting her house when her parents were at work, her brothers and sisters gone. Or into the park, or down to the beach. Two months of kissing before she would let him touch her *titas,* weeks more before she let him get his hand inside her jeans. He liked what he found there; boy, so did she.

She said his name then and he was in love.

Esteban doesn't disrespect her, he loves her, he wants to marry her, he told her so. One night under a tree out by the parking lot she stroked him off – *pobrecito* – his stuff on her warm brown thigh, but you knew it was going to happen, you knew he was going to get up in there once her jeans came off and he was so close he couldn't help himself and neither could she. That third month in her bed in her house when she let him in, he couldn't stop before he let loose inside her.

Now they will have to get married.

That's good, that's okay. He loves her, he wants this baby, he hopes it's a boy – a man becomes a man when he has a son – but he needs money.

So it's a good thing Lado is coming.

His *papi's jefe,* he owns the landscaping company Esteban's father works for. He does a lot more.

A lot more.

He is the gatekeeper for the Baja Cartel in Southern California.

A feared and respected man.

He's been giving Esteban some work. Not landscaping work. Little things at first. Take this message, be a lookout, ride along on this delivery, keep an eye on that corner. Little things, but Esteban did them well.

Esteban sees him coming, looks around, and gets into the car.

14

Here's how it works with lawyers and drug cartels.

If you're running drugs with a cartel and you get busted, the cartel sends you a lawyer. You aren't expected to shut up or keep secrets, you can go ahead and cooperate if that will get you off or buy you a shorter sentence. All you have to do is sit down with your cartel-appointed lawyer and tell him or her what you told the cops, so the cartel can make the necessary adjustments.

Then it's a numbers game.

You hire your lawyer and you pay him, win or lose. You pretty much expect to be found guilty; the issue is how much time you're going to do. Every drug offense has a sentencing guideline with a minimum and a maximum.

For every year under the guideline that your lawyer gets, you kick him a bonus, but you don't take any money away even if you get the max. You're a big boy, you knew the risks when you got into it. Your lawyer gets you what he can get you and that's it, no hard feelings, no recriminations, unless—

Your lawyer fucks up.

Your lawyer is so busy, or distracted, or indifferent, or just plain incompetent that he misses something that might have significantly reduced your sentence.

If that's the case, if the lawyer has cost you years of your life, you get to cost him years of his – to wit, the remaining ones. And if you're pretty high up in the cartel – an earner who's been bringing in seven figures a year – then you get to call on someone like Lado.

Such is the case with Roberto Rodriguez and Chad Meldrun.

Chad is a fifty-six-year-old criminal defense lawyer with a fine record, a nice home in Del Mar, a string of pretty girlfriends ten to fifteen years younger than himself—

'Don't you know they're only with you for your money?'

27

'Sure, so it's a good thing I have money.'

—and a wicked if somewhat anachronistic cocaine problem. Chad was pretty coked up and fucked out during Rodriguez's trial and he shined on a couple of motions in limine that might have reduced the prosecution's evidence to so much dog shit.

RR could have walked.

RR didn't. Only walk he took was in shackles to the bus for Chino. Now he's walking around the yard for fifteen to thirty. That's a lot of strolls to think about your lawyer fucking you up *on your own blow*. RR thinks long and hard about this, maybe five whole minutes, before he makes the call.

So now Lado is on his way to personally deliver justice, and he figures he'll get his kitten's paws wet. Lado likes the Discovery Channel and Animal Planet, and one thing he's learned is that mother leopards and cheetahs have to teach their young to hunt, the kittens don't know how to instinctively. So what the mother cats do is they wound an animal but don't finish it off. They bring it to their young so they learn how to kill.

That's nature.

Now he's going to break Esteban in – get him 'wet,' in the lingo.

The cartel needs soldiers up here. That was one of his missions when he got his green card and came here eight years ago.

Recruit.

Train.

28

Get ready for the day.

Now he drives to this lawyer's place.

He tells Esteban to grab the brown paper bag at his feet and open it. The kid does and pulls out a pistol.

Lado makes sure to notice his reaction.

The boy likes it. Likes the weight and heft in his hand.

Lado can see that.

15

Very nice place, this house.

Trimmed, tended lawn, manicured pebble walkway to the back of the house, to the kitchen door.

Esteban follows Lado down the pebbled path.

Lado rings the doorbell, even though they can see the lawyer standing at his kitchen island chopping onions. He sets down his knife and comes to the door.

'Yes?'

He looks annoyed, distracted, bothered maybe. Probably thinks they're *mujados* looking for work.

Lado puts one big hand to his chest and pushes him inside.

Esteban kicks the door shut behind them.

Now the lawyer looks scared. He glances at the knife on the cutting block but decides not to do that. He asks Lado, 'Who are you? What do you want?'

'Roberto Rodriguez asked me to visit you.'

The lawyer turns white. His legs start to shake a little and Esteban feels something he never felt before in his whole life—

Power.

Weight.

Some gravity on this American soil.

The lawyer's voice trembles. 'If it's money . . . let me get you some money.'

Lado snorts, 'Roberto could buy and sell you with what's in his pockets. What's money going to do for him in prison?'

'An appeal, we could—'

Lado shoots him, twice, in the legs.

The lawyer crumbles to the tile floor. Folds himself up and whimpers.

'Take your gun out,' Lado says to Esteban.

The boy takes the pistol from his pocket.

'Shoot him.'

Esteban hesitates.

'Never,' Lado says sternly, 'take your gun out if you're not going to shoot. Now shoot him. In the chest or the head, doesn't matter.'

The lawyer hears this and starts to beg. Tries to stand but his broken legs won't let him. Pulls himself across the kitchen floor on his forearms, leaving a streak of blood behind him, and Esteban thinks that his mother would hate to have to clean that up.

'Do it now,' Lado snaps.

Esteban don't feel powerful now.

He feels sick.

'If you don't,' Lado says, 'you're a witness. I don't leave witnesses.'

Esteban shoots.

The first bullet hits the lawyer in the shoulder, spinning him back down on the floor. Esteban steps up and makes sure this time, firing two bullets into his head.

On the way out, Esteban vomits on the pebbled path.

Later, that night, he lies with his head on Lourdes's belly and cries. Then he whispers into her tummy, 'I did it for you, *m'ijo*. I did it for you, my son.'

16

One Christmas

What was waiting under the tree for O were—

Boobs.

She was hoping for a bicycle.

This was during one of her (rare) Productive Periods, when she got herself a J-O-B, at the Quiksilver shop on Forest Avenue, and wanted green transportation to get back and forth from W-O-R-K.

So she came down in the morning (yeah, okay, it was eleven-thirty but still the fucking morning, yah), all excited like a kid even though she was nineteen at the time, and didn't see the shiny new bicycle she was hoping for but a shiny new envelope instead. Paqu was sitting cross-legged on the floor (this was during her Buddhist phase) and

Stepdad Three (Ben once observed that O was in the early phases of a Twelve Stepdad Program) was plopped in his easy chair grinning at her like the lascivious mouth-breathing cretin that he was, blissfully ignorant that he had one foot out the door anyway to make room for Four.

O opened the envelope to find a gift card from a cosmetic surgeon for:

'1 Complimentary Breast Augmentation.'

'This does mean, actually, *two* complimentary breast augmentations, right?' she asked Paqu.

'I'm sure it does, darling.'

'Because otherwise . . .' She drooped one shoulder down to illustrate, ultra-creeped out that Three was, like, assessing her bosom.

'Merry Christmas, my darling girl,' Paqu said, her face radiant with the glow of giving.

'I kind of like my breasts the way they are,' O said. Small, yes, but tasty, *yes,* and other people seem to like them, too. Given the right mellow weed, people have dined on them for *hours* . . .

'But, Ophelia, don't you want breasts like . . .'

She searches for the right word.

The word is 'mine,' O thought.

Don't you want boobs like *mine*? Mirror, mirror, on the wall, who has the nicest rack of all? Me, me, me, me. I walk through South Coast Plaza and make men hard from across the aisle. To affirm that I'm still attractive, not getting old, getting old getting old *not*. Don't you want to be beautiful like *me*?

Yeah, no.

'I really wanted a bicycle, Mom.'

Later, after three apple martinis over Xmas dinner at Salt Creek Inn, Paqu asked O if she was a lesbian. O confessed that she was. 'I'm a five-five bull dyke, Mom. Carpet munching and strap-ons are what I like, you bet.'

She traded the gift card to Ash for a bright red ten-speed.

Quit her job three weeks later anyway.

17

One day when Chon – then Johnny – was three years old, his father taught him a lesson about trust.

John Sr. was a founding member of the Association, the legendary group of Laguna beach boys who made millions of dollars smuggling marijuana before they fucked up and went to prison.

Big John lifted Little Johnny up to the living room fireplace mantel, held his arms out, and told him to jump. 'I'll catch you.'

Delighted, smiling, the little boy launched himself off the mantel, at which point Big John lowered his arms, did an *ole*, and Little Johnny crashed face-first on the floor. Dazed, hurt, bleeding from the mouth where a front tooth had gone into his lip, Chon learned the lesson his father had intended about trust:

Don't.

Ever.
Anyone.

18

Chon hasn't seen much of his father since the old man finished his fourteen-year federal stretch.

John came back to Laguna but by that time Chon was in the navy and they just sort of drifted apart. Chon bumps into him every once in a while at Starbucks or the Marine Room or just on the street and they exchange greetings and as much small talk as Chon can manage and that's about it.

There's no hostility; there's just no connection, either.

This doesn't bother Chon.

He doesn't yearn for it.

Chon's thinking is that twenty-some years ago his father fucked his mother, the sperm did their SEAL thing, and so what? His father was getting his nut, not signing up for Little League, fishing trips, or heart-to-heart talks. As for the fuckee, aka Mom, she liked dope a lot more than she liked Chon, and Chon gets this totally – he likes dope a lot more than he likes her.

Ben once observed that you could say Chon was 'raised by wolves,' except that wolves are warm-blooded mammals that care for their young.

Some backstory on Ben.

The missing Ben, the rarely present Ben.

Start with the genetic material—

Ben's father is a shrink, his mother a shrink.

Can we safely say he grew up in an over-analyzed home? Every word reconsidered, every action reinterpreted, every stone turned over for its hidden meaning.

What he craved most was privacy.

He loved (and loves) his parents. They are good, warm, caring people. People of the Left who came from People of the Left. His grand-parents were New York Jewish Communists, unreconstructed apologists for Stalin ('What was he *supposed* to do?') who sent their kids (Ben's parents) to a socialist summer camp in Great Barrington, Mass., where they met and formed an early association between sexuality and left-wing political dogma.

Ben's parents went from Oberlin to Berkeley, smoked pot, did acid, dropped out, dropped back in again, and ended up with comfortably lucrative psychotherapy practices in Laguna Beach.

Where they were among the very few Jews.

(One day Chon was bitching about being one of the few [former] military types in Laguna Beach, California, and Ben decided to take him up on it.

'You know how many Jews there are in Laguna?'
he asked.

'Is your mother Jewish?' Chon inquired.

'Yes.'

'Three.'

'Correct.')

Ben grew up listening to Pete Seeger and both
Guthries, Joan Baez, Dylan. Subscriptions to
*Commentary, Tikkun, The Nation, Tricycle, Mother
Jones.* Stan and Diane (Ben was instructed to
call them by their first names) were not upset
when they caught fourteen-year-old Ben with a
joint – just told him to smoke it in his room
and of course asked him endless questions: Was
he happy? Unhappy? Alienated? Not? Everything
okay at school? Was he confused about his
sexuality?

He was happy, unalienated, pulling a 4.0 and
relentlessly straight with a series of Laguna girls.

He just wanted to get high every now and then.

Stop analyzing everything.

Ben grew up in privilege but not wealth.

Nice but not luxurious house in the hills above
downtown Laguna, such as it is. Mom's and Pop's
offices were in the house, so he learned to come
in the side door after school so as not to walk in
on the patients in the waiting room.

He grew up Laguna cool.

Hit at the beach, smoked herb, walked around
barefoot. Hung at the basketball court, the volleyball court (was really good there, met Chon there,

partnered up and beat a lot of other teams there),
the playground.

Did well in school.

Genius at botany.

And business.

Ben went to Berkeley – of *course*.

Where else?

Double major – botany and marketing, and no
one asked what was up with that. Summa cum,
Phi Beta Kappa, honors thesis. But Ben was a
SoCal, not a NoCal (and these are not only
different states of mind, they are different countries) – he's sun, not fog, light, not heavy – so he
came home to Laguna.

Hooked up with Chon – when Chon was home –
and they played a lot more volleyball.

And went into business.

20

Every great company has an origin story and
here is Ben and Chonny's:

They're hanging out at the beach, Chon on
extended leave between his two hitches, and
they're playing volleyball on the court next to the
Hotel Laguna.

Ben and Chon are the kings of the court, and
why not? Two tall, lanky, athletic guys who make
a great team. Ben is the setter who thinks of the
game as chess, Chon is the spiker who goes for
the kill. They win a lot more often than they lose,

37

they have a good time, and tanned chicks in bikinis and suntan oil stop and watch them do it.

It's a good life.

So one day they're sitting on the sand post-match and start speculating about the future—

—what are they going to do—

and Ben brings up that old saw 'Do what you love and you'll never work a day in your life.'

Which sounds good to them.

Okay, what do we love? Chon asks.

Sex
Volleyball
Beer
Dope

They don't want to act in or make porn films, so sex is out. There are only about two guys in the whole world who make a decent living playing volleyball, the whole microbrewery thing is a bust, so . . .

Ben's been playing with hydro in his room.

A lot of trial and error, but lately he's actually produced some pretty potent stuff that he and Chon and O have smoked up.

And they love getting high, ergo . . .

Ben has the scientific and business knowledge and Chon has . . .

The baditude . . .

And a pedigree in this sort of thing, given his legacy.

'You were there when the Association tubed,' Ben observed. 'What went wrong?'

'Greed,' Chon said. 'Greed, carelessness, and stupidity.'

(Qualities that, to Ben, pretty much describe not only the defunct Association but the human species as a whole – greedy, stupid, and careless.)

Vowing to avoid greed, stupidity, and carelessness, Ben and Chon decided to go into the marijuana business. Not as smugglers or dealers, but as growers.

Their goal: to produce the best marijuana in the world.

This was the seed (we're getting there) of an idea, and, like any great idea, it all starts with the seed.

The best cannabis seed in the world comes from . . .

Afghanistan.

No ocean, no waves

But hellaciously fine cannabis seeds, the absolute premium of which is called—

The White Widow.

Coincidence or fate?

You decide.

21

The wine world is basically divided into red and white. (We ain't gonna go far with this – wine types are almost as hateful as tweekers.

Every great wine-tasting session should end with arsenic.)

The cannabis world is basically divided into *indica* and *sativa*.

Not to put too fine a point on it, *indicas* basically have a higher dose of CBDs than THCs and *sativas* have the reverse ratio.

Got it?

No, unless you're a blazer you don't, so some definitions (and no, there won't be a quiz at the end because we're talking about stoners here):

CBD is short for a substance in plants called cannabidiol. THC is the acronym of a substance in plants called tetrahydrocannabinol, aka Delta 9 tetrahydrocannabinol.

Unless you're Ben or Chon you don't need to know this shit, but to understand Ben and Chonny's you do need to get that the *indica* blends of cannabis – more CBI), less THC – produce a sleepy, heavy, tranquilizing kind of high. The *sativas* – more THC, less CBD – get your brain and genitals really cranking.

Or you can put it in terms of energy:

Indica = low energy. You're going to flop on the sofa and fall asleep to whatever is on TV because changing the channel requires too much effort.

Sativa = high energy. You're going to fuck your brains out on the sofa and then invent perpetual motion mechanics, or at least try to while you're repainting the living room.

So just as wine connoisseurs will yap endlessly

about this Merlot, that Beaujolais, grown from this or that fucking grape, stoners will likewise enthuse about different blends of *indica* and *sativa* – for their taste, their aroma, but mostly their effect. And finding the perfect blend of *indica* and *sativa* to suit the individual taste, that is the art of a master grower.

Just like great wine starts with the grape, great boo starts with the seed.

To wit, the White Widow.

The cannabis produced from the White Widow seed is the strongest in the world. The bud of that strain is 25 percent THC – the old Delta 9 is just about bursting out of it.

Expensive, hard to obtain, difficult to grow, and Worth it.

So on Chon's last tour of Stanland he came home with—

A bad case of PTLOSD

A burqa for O to wear on special occasions and

A bundle of White Widow seeds.

22

Giving White Widow seeds to Ben was like giving Michelangelo some paintbrushes and a blank ceiling and saying—

Go for it, dude.

What Ben did was take the White Widow and selectively breed it until it was even *stronger*. George Washington Ben Carver created a

Frankenstein seed, a mutant X-Men seed, a genetic freak of a seed.

This was a plant that could almost get up, walk around, find a lighter, and fire *itself* up. Read Wittgenstein, have deep conversations about the meaning of life with you, cocreate a television series for HBO, cause peace in the Middle East ('The Israelis and Palestinians could coexist in two parallel universes, sharing space but not time'). It took a strong man – or a strong woman, in O's case – to take more than one hit of the Ultra White Widow.

With that as his base, Ben started to create different blends of *indica* and *sativa,* all incredibly powerful, and he could customize them for each individual customer. Of which there evolved an increasing number as the word of mouth got around. Whatever it was you wanted to feel or not feel, Ben and Chon had dope for you.

One, then five, then ten, then thirty grow houses, all producing primo 420.

They became almost cultlike figures.

There developed such a devoted following with such a religious loyalty that they even gave themselves a name.

The Church of the Lighter Day Saints.

23

When it comes to the War On Drugs, Ben is a confirmed pacifist.

An Unconscientious Objector.

He simply refuses to participate.

'It takes two to fight,' he says, 'and I'm not fighting.'

Anyway, he doesn't believe that there is a War on Drugs.

'There is a War On Drugs Likely To Be Produced And/Or Consumed By People Of Color,' Ben allows.

White Drugs – alcohol, tobacco, pharmaceuticals – deal enough of those, you can overnight in the Lincoln bedroom. Black Drugs, Brown Drugs, Yellow Drugs – heroin, crack, boo – you get caught, you wake up every morning in your cell.

Chon disagrees. He doesn't think it's so much a racial thing as a Freudian thing. He thinks it has to do with anal/genital shame.

'It's about hemispheres,' Chon says one fine California day, standing on Ben's deck sucking on a spliff. 'Look at a globe, now analogize it to a human body. The northern hemisphere is like the head, the brain, the center of intellectual, philosophical, superego activity. The southern hemisphere is down there near the groin and the anus, where we do all those dirty, shameful, pleasurable id things. Where are most of your illicit – dig the word, B, 'illicit' – drugs produced? In that nasty dick, vagina, and asshole southern hemisphere.'

'But where,' Ben posits, 'are most of those same drugs consumed? In your brainy, moral, superego region.'

'Exactly,' Chon answers. 'That's why we need the drugs.'

Ben ponders this for a loooooonnng time, then

'So,' he says, 'you're saying that if we all took good shits and fucked a lot, there would be no drug abuse.'

'And,' Chon adds, 'no more war.'

'We'd both be out of work.'

'Okay.'

They laughed for a long time.

24

Stan and Diane never asked, never ask how their boy got so rich. That, they don't question or try to analyze. They don't do the financial forensics on how a twenty-five-year-old buys a four-million-dollar crib at Table Rock.

They're proud of him.

Not for *that,* for his social consciousness.

His social conscience.

And conscientiousness.

His Third World activism.

25

Which explains (sort of) where Ben is now.

Okay, Chon doesn't know exactly where Ben is now, which, with severed heads bouncing around the blogosphere, worries him a little, but—

—the boy does have a tendency to take care of

other people's business instead of his own. Ben has what they call a social conscience. Very aware, progressive dude. Chon likes that about him, *but*—

—bro tends to houdini for months at a time, saving some group of people from something. Wells to prevent cholera in the Sudan, mosquito nets to save kids in Zambia from malaria, observation teams to keep the army from slaughtering the Karen in Myan-myan-myan-mar.

Ben spreads his wealth.

Call it what you want

The Ben Foundation.

The Hydro Institute.

Dope Delivers

Green Is Green

Chon tries to tell him just send the money, let the cash fingers do the walking, stay and take care of business, but Ben is a handson kind of guy. Money isn't enough, he says, you have to commit your heart, soul, and body. Ben puts his money where his mouth is but also his mouth where his money is, so

—every few months he washes back up at Table Rock with dysentery—

—malaria and/or—

— Third World
Heartbreak—

(with which Chon is familiar)

– and Chon and O take him down to the best doctors at Scripps and then get him well until he finds another cause and then it's—

Gonzo again.
Off to rescue kids with tiny arms, big eyes, and
swollen stomachs.
Now Chon tells him via e-mail that he has a
problem right here at home. He forwarded the
video clip not to hurt Ben (he hates to hurt Ben),
but Ben has to know that there is bad shit
happening *here*.
People being turned into Pez dispensers.

26

Ben's disembodied head
floats in the ether.
Skype.
Blurred background behind the focus on his
face.
Unkempt brown hair.
Brown eyes.
His lips slightly out of synch, a broken second's
lag behind the sound as he says,
'Okay, I'm coming home.'

27

O is happy
that Ben is coming back.
Ben, her other bookend
The two men – Ben and Chon—
who mean something in her life.
The only two who ever have.

46

28

Ben is warm wood, Chon is cold metal
Ben is caring, Chon indifferent
Ben makes love, Chon fucks.
She loves them both.
What to do, what to do?

29

When O gets up that morning (okay, afternoon), she looks out the window and sees a tall woman with close-cropped silver hair get into a BMW and pull out of the driveway.

'Who was that?' O asks Paqu when she walks into the kitchen to look for the Cocoa Puffs that Paqu has probably thrown out. (O hijacks the shopping list that Paqu gives Maria and adds items like Cocoa Puffs, Lucky Charms, Hostess CupCakes, self-heating lubricating gel, and Jimmy Dean sausage biscuits. But then Paqu goes on patrol in the pantry and throws these things out, save for the gel, which O whips into her room the second Maria comes back with the groceries.)

'That's Eleanor, my life coach,' Paqu says. 'She's *won*derful.'

'Your . . .'

'Life coach.'

This is just 2G2BT. This makes O really happy. Her skin gets all tingly as she asks, 'Just what does a life coach actually *do*, Mom?'

Sure enough, Paqu gave the Puffs the heave, so O has to settle for Frosted Mini-Wheats, then scans the fridge for real, actual milk, not the skimmed or 1 percent shit that Moms insists on stocking when she's not completely antidairy, which is apparently now, so O pours the cereal into a bowl and eats it dry, with her fingers, a small measure of revenge.

'Well, Eleanor thinks I have the makings of a life coach my*self*,' Paqu answers, placing some flowers into a tall, skinny vase. 'So she's going to help me actualize that potential.'

The potential actualization of that potentiality gets O even zingier. 'So your life coach is coaching you to be a life coach.'

So you can coach other people to be life coaches. O almost hustles out the door right then because she just can't wait to report this circle jerk of life coaching to Ben (Ben's coming home!) and Chon.

Paqu ignores the question. 'She's truly amazing.'

'What happened to the skin-care product thing?'

'Superficial, don't you think?' Paqu looks at the flower arrangement and smiles with self-satisfaction. Then she has a revelation. 'Darling! *You* could study to be a life coach, *too*! Then we could be mother-and-daughter life coaches!'

'But then you'd have to come clean that you have a daughter over the age of ten,' O says, shoveling Mini-Wheats into her mouth.

Paqu peruses her with what O guesses is meant to be life coach – level discernment.

'Of course, you'd have to do something about that hair,' Paqu says. 'And the . . . "body art."'
'Maybe I could start as a "life cheerleader."'
Rah.

30

Chon sits in the black leather chair and watches the inauguration of the new president of the United States.

Who reaches out a hand to the Muslim world.

Chon gets that – he's reached out to the Muslim world a few times himself.

It's good Ben is coming back. The new prez agrees. He's telling the thousands in attendance and the millions watching on television that the feeding frenzy at the trough is over, the orgy has been put on indefinite hiatus, the Third World is closer than you think, in both time and space.

Recession.

Depression.

Repression.

Whichever word you use, there's a smaller pie to slice up and the knives are out. (See Clip, Video.) Layoffs, lop-offs, the market self-correcting. Companies becoming more efficient and the Baja Cartel is at the cutting edge (oof).

'How do you think we should respond?' Ben asks in the Skype session.

'Reach out to the Mexican world.'

'Violence is not necessarily the answer,' Ben says.

49

It's not necessarily *not* the answer, either, Chon thinks.

This violent state of mind.

This violent state of mine.

As he watches the old president – aka the Sock Puppet – wave and get on the helicopter.

The last time someone tried to muscle Ben and Chonny's it was a biker gang. Those boys picked up one of their retailers and beat him to death with a tire iron as a message that Ben and Chon could no longer do retail in the greater San Diego area.

Ben, natch, was off doing good somewhere, so this is how Chon took care of it.

31

Flashback:

Chon rolls down the 5 in his classic black '66 pony.

Pointed toward Fun Dog.

Etymology:

San Diego

Sun Diego

Sun Dog

Fun Dog

In the backseat under a blanket sleeps a Remington Model 870 SPS Super Slug pump action, 12-gauge shotgun with a synthetic cantilevered slug and a rubberized pistol grip that 'advances deerleveling technology to farther reaches and smaller group sizes than ever before possible.'

Right now it's resting up for the big business meeting.

32

Chon likes to keep meetings short.

Learned that in a book, *Things They Don't Teach You at Harvard Business School.*

A short meeting is a good meeting.

He drives down to Dago, finds the house in Golden Hill he's looking for, and parks on the street. Wakes the shotgun up ('We're there'), crosses said street, and knocks on the door.

Tire Iron opens it. Big wooly motherfucker, heavy hairy shoulders showing under the wifebeater.

Chon puts the shotgun to T.I.'s throat and pulls the trigger.

Guy's head goes ballpark.

(*Fun* Dog!)

Something they don't teach you at Harvard Business School.

'Savages, How to Deal With.'

Savagely.

33

Continuing in flashback mode:
Chon goes back to the Tuna—

51

Etymology:

(And, by the way, Chon really likes the word 'etymology,' the etymology of which is Greek and means 'in the true sense.' Hmmmm . . .)

Laguna, rhymes with

Tuna—

Holes up with a freaking arsenal, tells O not to come around until the biker gang responds.

They don't.

He never hears from them again except by word on the California Bongo Drum Communications System that they've decided to get out of the herb business and focus their efforts on meth.

A sound management decision.

Do not expand horizontally until you have achieved maximum vertical capacity.

Also: do not fuck with someone until you know exactly who the fuck you're fucking with.

And then don't do it.

34

'Don't fuck with people at all'

Is a central tenet of Ben's personal as well as business philosophy.

Ben is a self-described Baddhist, i.e., a 'bad Buddhist,' because he sometimes eats meat, gets angry, rarely meditates, and definitely does consciousness-altering substances. But the *basics* of Buddhism, Ben is down with—

Do no harm

Which Ben articulates as

Don't fuck with people.

And he doesn't think the Dalai Lama would argue with that.

In addition to the interest-accruing deposits in the karma bank, it's been a very successful business strategy, the very foundation of the very successful Ben and Chonny's brand.

A brand it is.

You go into B&C's as either a customer or a sales partner, you know exactly what you're getting:

As a customer—

Top-o'-the-line, not-to-be-bettered, safe, healthy, organic, prime hydro at a fair price

As a sales partner—

a superb product that sells itself
profit participation
excellent working conditions
day care
health care

Yes, health care, written through Ben's corporation that e-markets Third World crafts made by Third World women.

You see, Ben does adhere to the Buddhist belief in making a 'right living,' which mixes in quite nicely with his childhood socialist indoctrination and his somewhat Reaganite entrepreneurial sense.

Not for Ben the rigid, top-down vertical integration of the Baja Cartel. B&C (and the ampersand is everything, in Ben's opinion) has a loosely organized, horizontal, flow-out ('Money doesn't shoot upward to then trickle down, it flows *out*') pseudostructure that allows for maximum freedom and creativity.

Ben's logic on this is that it's impossible to organize marijuana dealers anyway (for reasons that are probably obvious), so why try to herd (cool) cats when they do better on their own, anyway. So—

You wanna sell dope? Cool. You don't? Cool. You wanna sell a lot? Cool. You wanna sell a little? Cool. Maternity leave? Cool. Paternity leave? Cool. You set your own targets, make your own budgets, set your own salary, it's *all* cool. You just order however much you want from the Mother Ship and then do your own thing.

This simple philosophy, plus the care he takes in growing his primo product, has made Ben a very rich young man.

The King of Hydro.

The King of Cool.

35

There are, of course, some critics – and Ben is one of them – who will say that Ben can be Ben because Chon is Chon.

54

Ben acknowledges his own hypocrisy on this issue.

(He is nothing but self-aware and self-analytical. See:

Ben, parentage of.)

He and Chon even have a noun for it:

'Hydrocrisy.'

The hydrocrisy is obvious – Ben strives to be nonviolent and honest in a business that is violent and dishonest.

'But it doesn't have to be,' Ben has argued.

'But it is,' Chon countered.

'But it shouldn't be.'

'Okay, but so what?'

Well, so what is that Ben has taken 99 percent of the violence and dishonesty out of his business, but that other 1 percent is—

—where Chon comes in.

Ben doesn't need to know what Ben doesn't need to know. 'You're the American public,' Chon tells him.

And Chon has ample experience with that.

36

Guys dying in Iraq and Afghanistan and the headlines are about

Anna Nicole Smith.

Who?

Exactly.

Ben watches CNN in the airport.
On his way home from the Bongo Congo.
Etymology—

The Congo River runs through it, and
It used to be called the Belgian Congo, and
It's fucking nuts there.

Otherwise known as the Democratic Republic
of the Congo.
What was Ben the Baddhist doing there?
Funding psychotherapy clinics for rape victims.
Traumatized women, multiply raped and often
mutilated – first by rebel soldiers, then by the
soldiers who were sent to protect them from
the previous set of soldiers. So Green Is Green
writes checks for health clinics and counselors,
for pregnancy and STD tests, and—
—get this—
—for instructors to go out to the soldiers and
hold workshops to teach that rape and mutilation
are—
wrong.
Ben leaves the plastic molded chair to hit the
porcelain in the men's room again because he
contracted more in the Congo than just the usual
Third World Heartbreak and he really hopes it
isn't dysentery (again).

He sits Luther-like on the john and, in fact, (re)considers his own theology because—

—while he knows as a Baddhist that men who rape and cut up women should be re-educated not to do that, he also has this impulse that the more effective thing to do would be to just—

—shoot the fuckers.

He knows (ever self-reflective) that there's more to it than that.

Maybe he's just sick and tired but he's also
sick
and
tired
of seemingly *everything* these days. He feels
ennui
depression
adrift in his life. Purposeless, perhaps because

—dig a well in the Sudan and the *janjaweed* come in and shoot the people anyway

—buy mosquito nets and the boys you save grow up to
    —rape women

—set up cottage industries in Myanmar and the army
    —steals them and uses the women as slaves
  and

Ben is starting to be afraid that he is starting to share Chon's opinion of the human species
that people are basically
shit.

And now this

Ben thinks as he goes back to the first-class lounge and gets himself an herbal tea.

The BC sends out atrocity videos as a business tool in the heretofore (relatively) pacifist marijuana industry.

Nice.

What next?

He doesn't even want to think about that.

Yeah, but you're going to have to, he tells himself, because you're going to have to respond to it. Chon has a response in mind (well, in hand), but the truth is that there's no way they're going to outgun the Baja Cartel. And even if they could, Ben's not sure that he wants to.

Ben's not sure of anything right now.

He hears them announce his flight.

39

Threatened with eviction and/or a limit on her platinum card, O agrees to join a life coaching session with Paqu.

Eleanor comes to the house.

'Is she like Domino's?' O asks Paqu. 'If she doesn't deliver a new life in twenty minutes, it's free?'

'That will be enough of that.'

So O joins Paqu on the sofa as Eleanor, her silver

hair set off beautifully by a deep-lavender silk blouse, passes out file cards as she says, 'Three is a very powerful number in our culture and collective psyches, so we are going to use the power of three to enhance our personal power.'

'And there are three of us,' O observes.

'Very sharp, Ophelia,' Eleanor says.

O winces.

Eleanor continues, 'The difference between a goal and a dream is a plan of action, so on these cards, I want you to write down three goals you have for yourself for today, and the three achievable steps you will take today to make each one happen.'

Paqu writes:

—Become physically stronger

—Progress toward becoming a life coach

—Prepare a meal that will nourish me physically and spiritually.

O writes:

—Have mind-blowing multiple orgasm.

'I asked for *three* things,' Eleanor says.

'If I get it right, it *will* be three things,' O answers.

Eleanor's tough, though. She doesn't pull two and a half bills an hour from a slough of jaded SOC trophy wives by being a wimp. She levels her gaze at O and asks, 'And what three achievable steps will you take to move you toward your goal?'

O nods and reads:

—Put C batteries on Mom's shopping list

—Find some time for myself

—Think about the pool boy

They pick Ben up at John Wayne Airport.

Chon thinks you gotsta love an airport named for a draft-dodging movie war hero cowboy who trademarked his gay, pigeon-toed mince into a macho money machine. Bought half of south Orange County back in the day, practically owned Newport Beach, like fuck the movies, real estate is where the treasure be.

Aaarrrrhh.

All those cats – Wayne, Hope, Crosby – they bought up big chunks of the California Dream – Newport Beach, Palm Springs, Del Mar – and sold it like they sold their celluloid fantasies. Sunshine, sailing, golf.

Lotsa golf.

Martinis on the green, sly in-jokes, thousand-dollar hookers waiting in the carts, blow-job bets on birdies, bogeys, whatever rich white guy my small dick isn't as small as your small dick crapola. Get your ball on the green, on the green, on the green green green.

Losers get the sand traps.

Iraq. Stanland.

What's the club they use to get out of the sand traps? The wedge? Chon wonders. Yeah, as if, wouldn't that be nice. Stuck in the Stan, just have your caddy hand you your trusty wedge, take a sweet swing, and you're out on the green.

Martinis and blowies for everyone, my good man.

He and Ben played golf once. Took the pony down to Torrey Pines, got *ripped* on speed, and did nine holes in like seven and a half minutes, whacking at that ball like Cossacks swinging at heads. Didn't replace their divots, of which there were *many*. Ran from shot to shot like they were dodging sniper fire. Hit the ground and roll, come up swinging. Until an indignant steward came and tossed them off.

Thrown off the beautiful greens.

Off the Dream.

The Duke, Der Bingle, and the Bobster don't want you here anymore.

Ben wanted Chon to object – I'm a war veteran, I fought to protect your right to shoot eighteen holes on a beautiful California morning by the sea by the sea by the beautiful sea you and me you and me oh how happy we'll be. I bled for these holes. Without men like me, the clubhouse whores would be wearing burqas, my friend.

But Chon wouldn't do it. Refused to summon up the righteous indignation. Truth was, he *didn't* go to Stanland to defend his country club. He went because he was already in the SEALs when those cocksuckers flew airplanes into the WTC.

He didn't say that to the steward, though. Guy was already cardiac-paddle-ready, so Chon just said, 'Keep it green,' and left without further incident.

Anyway, now he's at John Wayne Airport. You fly into Orange County, they let you know what you've gotten into, pilgrim. Don't be fooled by the hip surfer thing, you are in Rich Republicanland and you'd better behave accordingly or they'll let the Duke loose on you.

As if.

Just a short while ago the Republicans were objects of fear and hatred – now they're just pathetic assholes. Barry took them to the paint and cut their throats. (O-*BAM*-a!) Now they walk around like white frat boys in Bed-Stuy, talking tough to show they aren't scared as the urine streams down their chinos into their cordovans. Obama has these dweebs so turned around all they can do is get behind some fat junkie DJ, a gibberish-spewing PsychoBimbette from the Far North, and a tele-dork who gives adrenaline-crazed, 1950s-style 'chalk talks' (speaking of little white dicks) like some health-class instructor in a sex-offender unit.

Chon has a mental vid-clip of this clown choking on a chicken bone in a restaurant, rolling on the floor while the black and Spanish waiters and busboys fall all over each other hustling to dial 511.

Of course the Dems will find some dazzlingly random way to fumble at the goal line; they always do ('What did you say your name was, darlin'? Monica?'). In the meantime Chon can't wait – can't *wait* – for the inevitable moment one of these clowns chokes on an open mike and calls Obama a nigger. It's going to happen, you *know* it's going to happen, it's just a matter of time and it will be a blast to see the dazed befuddled expression on that pasty stupid face as he realizes his career is deader than a Kennedy.

POSTMORTEM CAREER COUNSELOR
And your career died how?

CHUCKLEHEAD
I called Obama a nigger.

POSTMORTEM CAREER COUNSELOR
(Incredulous pause)
Wow.

In the meantime, the GOP just settles for other kinds of buffoonery. Chon's personal fave is the guy of South Goober banging the *chica* in South America while claiming he's on a hiking trip in the Appalachians (on 'Naked Hiking Day,' no less).

Then crying about it.

The other thing about Republicans – they cry on TV these days like a twelve-year-old girl who didn't get invited to a birthday party. ('It's okay, Ashley – Brittany's a jerk – everybody *loves* you.')

Republicans didn't used to cry.

Democrats cried and Republicans mocked them for it.

The way it should be.

Ask John Wayne.

Chon used to hate Democrats as weak-kneed yuppie hypocrites, a party of closeted gay men too gutless to come out and stand up for who they are. He still does, but since Iraq – since the Sock Puppet got his leash yanked by Mr Wilson – who Chon *really* hates are Republican politicians. Not to put too fine a point on it, Chon thinks they should be hunted down like rabid dogs, shot, and tossed into a common pit, with lime poured over their rotting corpses so they don't emerge some Halloween night like the zombies they would otherwise become.

Anyway . . .

41

They find Ben in baggage claim waiting for his green duffel bag, like he's still some college kid coming home from a field trip to Costa Rica.

He looks thin like he always does when he comes home. His skin, in that particularly weird, Third World way, is simultaneously tan and pale – dark from the sun with a sub-layer of infection-induced white underneath. What is it this time? Anemia? Hep? Some parasite that's crept under his toenail into his bloodstream?

Bilharzia.

Ben sees them and smiles.

Big white even teeth.

In a different generation Ben would have been in the Peace Corps. Shit, Ben would have been the

64

director of the Peace Corps, played touch football with Jack and Bobby on the lawn at Hyannis Port, out sailing on the yacht. Tan and smiling. A life of vigor, moral and physical.

But that was a different generation.

O runs up to him, throws her arms around his shoulders, wraps her legs around his waist. It's no prob, she weighs, like, nothing.

'Bennnnnnnnnnnnnn!!!!!!!!'

The other passengers turn and look.

Ben holds her up with one arm, pivots, and extends his other hand to Chon.

'Hey.'

'Hey.'

His bag comes down the conveyor belt. Chon picks it up, hefts it on his shoulder, and they walk out past the statue of

The Duke—

And, by the way—

Fuck *him*.

42

The Coyote Grill

In south Laguna Beach

Just an exterior stairway up from Table Rock and the condo.

They sit out on the balcony. A rectangle of blue Pacific down below them, fishing boats cruising the edge of the kelp beds, Catalina lying fat and lazy (a spoiled house cat) on the edge of the world.

Nice nice.

Sun shining and the air smells of fresh salsa.

It's Ben's favorite place when he's home. His hang. But he doesn't eat a lot today, just pushes his food around the plate and nibbles on a tortilla and Chon thinks he probably has some gut malady. Rumbling intestines and frequent trips to the john. Load up on magazines because Ben is going to get a lot of reading done.

Chon has a burger. He hates Mexican food. His opinion is that all Mexican food is the same, it's just wrapped differently.

O eats like a horse.

Big plate of nachos with chicken, fish tacos with yellowtail, rice, and black beans. Having Ben home gives her even more than her usual ravenous appetite. (Her two men around her.) It's almost disgusting watching her shovel the food into her mouth. Paqu would hemorrhage through her fucking ears if she saw this.

Which would make O even hungrier.

Ben orders an iced tea but Chon tells him clear liquids are better. You have the trots, only drink fluids you can see through. Ben gets a lemonade and mostly just chews on the ice.

'Where have you been?' O asks between gulps.

'All over,' Ben answers. 'First I was in Myanmar.'

'Myan . . . ?'

'—mar,' Ben says. 'Used to be Burma. Go to Thailand and take a left? I ended up in Congo.'

'What was in Congo?' Chon asks.

Ben gives him that *Apocalypse Now* look. Brando before the Pudding Pops.

The *horror*.

43

Home home.

Welcome home.

Ben walks into the big living room and instantly starts checking it out, doing a mental inventory to see what vodka-and-speed-propelled damage Chon has done.

But the place looks good.

Pristine.

'You brought a cleaner in,' Ben says.

'One of Paqu's anal retentives,' O says.

'It looks nice,' Ben says. 'Thanks.'

Paqu's house cleaners generally go in one of two directions – have nervous breakdowns and quit, hopefully stealing something of value on their way out the door; or are obsessive-compulsives who are totally into meeting her impossible standards. O brought one of the latter types in to sterilize Ben's crib.

Now they sit on the sofa and smoke up. Look out at the ocean. Look out at the ocean. Look out at the ocean . . .

Chon says he's going for a training swim.

That means a *long* swim, couple of miles at least, plus the walk back. He leaves the room, comes back with his trunks on, and says, 'Later.'

They watch him walk out onto the beach and jump into the water.

No toe-dipping for Chon.

44

Or for O.

'How long has it been,' she asks Ben, 'since you've had a woman?'

'A few months.'

'That's too long.'

She kneels in front of him, unzips his fly, licks butterfly wings up and down him. He stops her and asks, 'How does Chon feel about this?'

'It isn't his tongue, isn't his mouth.' And swallows him deep, slides her lips up and down his beautiful warmwood cock, feels him harden, loves her power to make that happen, bobs her head up and down, knowing he'll dig the sight of that, guys love the sight of that (seeming) submission; she sees his fingers grip the sofa cushion.

'You want to come in my mouth,' she asks, 'or in my pussy?'

'In you.'

She takes his hand and leads him into the bedroom. Pulls her dress up over her head, slides her panties down her legs, and kicks them off. Takes off his shirt, his jeans, his boxers and pulls him down on top of her.

'Are you wet?' Ben asks.

Pure Ben, always considerate. Ben never wants to hurt anyone.

'God, yes. Feel me.'

Opens herself to let him see

her glistening.

'God, O.'

'You want to fuck me, Ben?'

'Oh yes.'

'Fuck me, sweet Ben.'

Sweet sweet Ben so slow and gentle so strong and gentle, so warm so fucking fucking fucking warm, his brown eyes looking into hers questioning, asking if this pleasure can be real asking if this pleasure can be really found and his smile an answer, the answer yes because his smile makes her come a small one, the first small wave.

The mermaid on her arm strokes his back, the green sea vines entwine him and hold him to her, sweet sticky trap, dolphins surfing on his spine as he rides her, their salty sweat meeting and mixing, slicking them together, sticking them together, little frothy white bubbles joining his cock and her cunt.

O loves his hardsoft cock in her, loves gripping his shoulders as he moves in and out; in his ear she whispers, 'I missed this.'

'Me, too.'

'Sweet, sweet, sweet Ben, fucking me.'

The 'me' triggers another climax, it's the 'me' of it, this beautiful, wonderful, sweet, loving man, it's 'me' he wants to fuck, his beautiful warm brown eyes looking into 'mine,' his hands on my back his cock in my pussy.

She comes again and tries to slow down but can't, but can't, she gives up on the control she wanted to make this slow for him make it last for him but can't and she jacks her hips to push her clit into his pubic bones and circles her hip to grind it there his cock deep inside her.

'Oh, Ben. Oh!'

Her fingers, a crab scuffling across the wet sand, race down to his ass, search for and find the crevice, a tidal pool, she pushes a finger in and hears him groan and feels him shoot deep inside her his back muscles shudder, and then again, and then he falls on her.

The mermaid smiles.

The dolphins fall asleep.

So do Ben and O.

45

Ben gently untangles himself from her moist arms.

Gets out of bed, puts on his jeans and shirt, and steps into the living room. Through the big window he sees Chon sitting out on the deck. Ben goes to the fridge, grabs two Coronas, and goes out.

Hands Chon a beer, leans against the white metal railing, asks, 'Good swim?'

'Yeah.'

'No sharks?'

'Not that I saw.'

No surprise – sharks are afraid of Chon. Predators recognize each other.

Ben says, 'We make the deal.'

'Mistake.'

'What,' Ben says. 'You worried their dick is bigger than our dick now?'

'*Our* dick?'

'Okay, our *dicks*. Our collective dick. Our joint dick.'

'Redundant,' Chon says. 'Let's just keep our dicks separate.'

'Okay, they won,' Ben says. 'And what did we lose? We got out of a business we want to get out of anyway. I'm telling you, Chon, I'm bored with it. Time to move on. Next.'

'They think we're afraid of them.'

'We are.'

'Separate dicks?' Chon says. 'I'm not.'

'We're not all you,' Ben says. 'We don't all chew up and spit out fifteen terrorists before breakfast. I don't want a war. I didn't get into this thing to fight wars, kill people, get people killed, get their heads lopped off. This used to be a pretty mellow gig, but if it's going to get to this level of savagery, forget it. I don't want to be a part of it. They think we're afraid of them? Who fucking cares? This isn't fifth grade, Chon.'

Yeah, it isn't, Chon thinks. It isn't a pride thing, an ego thing, or a dick thing.

Ben just doesn't get how these people think. He can't wrap his rational head around the reality that these people will interpret his reasonableness as weakness. And when they see weakness, when they smell fear, they attack.

They pour it on.

But Ben will never get that.

'We can't beat the cartel in a shooting war, the math just doesn't pencil,' Ben says.

Chon nods. He has guys he could recruit, good people who can take care of business, but the BC has an army. Still, what are you going to do? Grab the KY, bend over the railing? Prison love?

'This was just a way of making a living,' Ben says. 'My balls aren't attached to it. We have some money stashed. Cook Islands, Vanuatu . . . We can live comfortably. Maybe it's time to put our focus somewhere else.'

'Bad time for a start-up, Ben.'

The market a bobsled run. The credit stream a *barranca*. Consumer confidence at an all-time low. End of capitalism as we know it.

'I'm thinking alternative energy,' Ben says.

'Windmills, solar panels, that kind of shit?'

'Why not?' Ben asks. 'You know how they're making those fourteen-dollar laptops for kids in Africa? What if you could make a ten-dollar solar panel? Change the fucking world.'

Ben still doesn't get—

—Chon thinks—

—that you don't change the world.

It changes you.

For example—

46

Three days after Chon gets back from the Rack he and O are sitting in a restaurant in Laguna when a waiter drops a tray.

Clatter.

Chon dives under the table.

Down there on all fours reaching for a weapon that isn't there and if Chon were capable of social self-consciousness he'd be humiliated. Anyway, it's tough to get nonchalantly back in your chair after diving under the table with a restaurant full of people staring at you and the adrenaline is still juicing his nervous system so he stays down there.

O joins him.

He looks over and there she is, eyeball to eyeball with him.

'A little jumpy, are we?' she asks.

'A tad.'

Good word, 'tad.' The one-syllable jobs are usually the best.

O says, 'As long as I'm on my hands and knees . . .'

'There are laws, O.'

'Slave to conformity.' She sticks her head out from under the table and asks, 'Could we get a refill on the water, please?'

The waiter brings it to her, under the table.

'I kind of like it down here,' she says to Chon. 'It's like having a fort when you were a kid.'

She reaches up, grabs the menus, and hands one to Chon. After a few moments of perusal she says, 'I'm going to go with the chicken Caesar salad.'

The waiter, a young surfer-type dude with a perfect tan and perfect white smile, squats beside the table. 'May I tell you about our specials?'

Gotta love Laguna.

Gotta love O.

47

Ben wants peace.

Chon knows

You can't make peace with savages.

48

O wakes up from her nap, gets dressed, and comes out onto the deck.

If the girl feels awkward about being in the presence of two guys she's simul-doing, she doesn't show it. Probably because she doesn't feel it. Her thinking on this is basic and arithmetical:

More love is better than less love.

She hopes they feel the same way, but if they don't—

Oh well.

Ben and Chon decide to roll down to Dickyville.

Etymology:

San Clemente, home of the former Western White House of
Richard Nixon
Aka Dick Nixon
Aka Tricky Dick
Dickyville
Sorry.
O wants to go with.

'Yeah, not a good idea,' Ben says. They've never involved her in the business before.

Chon feels the same way – it's a line he doesn't think they should cross.

'I really want to go,' O says.

Still—

'I don't want to be alone.'

'Could you be with Paqu?'

'I don't want to be alone.'

'Got it.'

They roll down to Dickeyville.

49

To see Dennis.

They pull off at a parking lot on the beach. The railroad track runs right past it. Ben and O sometimes take that train just for the hell of it, sit and watch dolphins and sometimes whales out the window.

Dennis is already there. He gets out of his Toyota Camry and walks over to the Mustang. In his late forties, Dennis has sandy hair that is just starting to thin arid packs thirty excess pounds on his six three frame because he can't seem to drive *past* a drive-*thru* these days. In fact, there's a Jack in the Box just across the 5 . . . Anyway, he's a handsome guy except for the stomach that hangs over his belt.

He's surprised to see Ben, because usually he meets solo with Chon.

Then he usually swings by Jack in the Box.

He's even more surprised to see this chick he doesn't know. 'Who's this?'

O says, 'Anne Heche.'

'No, you're not.'

'Well, you asked who I was.'

Ben says, 'She's a friend of ours.'

Dennis doesn't like it at all. 'Since when do we invite friends to these parties?'

'Well, it's my party, Dennis,' Ben says.

'And I'll cry if I want to,' O adds.

'Get in,' Ben says.

Dennis gets into the front passenger seat. Chon and O sit in the back.

'I shouldn't be seen in the same zip code with you guys,' Dennis whines.

'You don't seem to mind when I have your gift bag,' Chon says. He and Dennis meet once a month. Chon arrives with a satchel full of cash and leaves without it. Dennis arrives with no satchel full of cash and leaves with one.

Then he usually swings by Jack in the Box.

'Would you prefer we come to the office?' Ben

76

asks, the office being the federal building in downtown San Dog where the DEA is headquartered.

Where Dennis is a big deal in the antidrug task force.

'Jesus, what has your panties in a wad?' Dennis isn't used to seeing this side of Ben – well, he isn't used to seeing much of Ben at all, but when he does, the guy is normally pretty congenial. And Chon – well, forget it – Chon *always* looks jacked up.

'You have intel on the Baja Cartel?' Ben asks. 'Hernan Lauter?'

Dennis chuckles. 'That's about all I do.'

Yeah, because he's sure as shit not putting any effort into scoping out Ben and Chon's operation. Every once in a while, they'll toss him a stash or an old grow house, just to keep him upwardly mobile on the promotion ladder, but that's about it.

'Why?' he asks, thinking he's about to get a nugget maybe he can use. 'The BC making a move on you guys?'

He has it on his radar.

He's not fucking stupid.

There've been pings all over the place, including a viral video featuring seven decapitated dope dealers.

Talk about your hostile takeovers.

And now Ben is going to come whining about it?

Then the dime drops.

'Wait a second,' he says to Ben, 'if you're here to negotiate a payment reduction because the BC is cutting a slice off you, forget it. Your overhead is your overhead, not mine.'

A train comes busting down the track.

The Metrolink, which runs from Oceanside just down the road all the way up to L.A. The conversation stops because they can't hear each other anyway, then Ben says, 'I need to know everything you know about Hernan Lauter.'

'Why?' Dennis asks, relieved anyway that they're not trying to shuck him. Dennis has bills.

'"Why" is not your issue,' Chon says. 'Your issue is "what."'

So tell us what you know about Hernan.

The head of the Baja Cartel.

50

Dennis runs it down for them.

It starts not in Baja but in Sinaloa.

A mountainous region of western Mexico that has the right altitude, soil acidity, and rainfall to grow the poppy. For generations, the Sinaloan *gomeros* – Spanish slang for opium farmers – cultivated the crop, processed it into opium, and sold it to an American market, at first made up mostly of Chinese railroad workers, along the southwest border region of Texas, New Mexico, Arizona, and California.

The American government at first tolerated the

trade, but then declared opium illegal and brought some, albeit ineffectual, pressure on the Mexican government to suppress the *gomeros*.

But during WWII, the American government did a complete 180. Desperately needing opium with which to make morphine, and cut off from the usual supplies in Afghanistan and the Golden Triangle, the government went down to Mexico to beg them to produce more, not less, opium. In fact, we built narrow-gauge railways for the *gomeros* to get their crop down from the mountains faster. The *gomeros* responded by putting more and more acreage into poppy cultivation. Therefore, during the 1940s, the economy of Sinaloa became dependent on the opium trade, and the *gomeros* grew into rich and powerful landholders.

After the war the U.S., faced with a bad heroin problem at home, goes back down to Mexico and insists that they stop growing the poppy. The Mexicans are, to say the least, a little confused, but also concerned because the Sinaloans – not just the rich *gomeros* but the *campesinos*, peasant farmers who work the land – are economically addicted to the poppy.

No worries, says the American mafia. Bugsy Siegel goes to Sinaloa and assures the *gomeros* that the mob will buy as much opium as they can produce. The *pista secreta* – the illegal drug trade – commences, and rival *gomeros* start to fight each other for turf. Culiacán, the major city in Sinaloa, becomes known as 'Little Chicago.'

Enter Richard Nixon.

In 1973, Nixon creates the Drug Enforcement Administration and sends DEA agents – most of them former CIA – down to Sinaloa to shut down the *gomeros*. Then 1975 sees Operation Condor, in which DEA agents, with the Mexican army, bomb, burn, and defoliate vast acreage of poppy cultivation in Sinaloa, displacing thousands of peasants and wrecking the economy.

And get this, get this, the Mexican cop running their side of the operation – the man pointing fingers at what to bomb and burn, whom to arrest – is the second-largest opium producer in Sinaloa, a truly evil genius named Miguel Angel Alvarado, who uses Condor to destroy his rivals.

Alvarado gathers the chosen survivors in a restaurant in Guadalajara – guarded by the army and the *federales* – and he creates el Federacion, the Federation, and divides Mexico up into *plazas,* or territories, to wit—

The Gulf, Sonora, and Baja, with himself, based in Guadalajara, at its head.

Alvarado, a genuine business revolutionary, also takes them out of the opium business and puts them into delivering Colombian cocaine through the Mexican back door.

The front door being Florida. Miami. Where the DEA was putting most of its efforts. The poor schmucks left in Mexico were screaming about the cocaine deliveries – again, guarded by the army and the police – but DC told them to keep their stupid mouths shut if they knew what was good for them, because they'd already announced that they'd won the drug war in Mexico.

Mission accomplished.

El Federacion, in its three plazas, made billions of dollars during the eighties and nineties, gaining so much wealth and power that it became almost a shadow government, enmeshed into the police, the military, even the president's office. By the time DC woke up and admitted the reality, it was too late. El Federacion was a major power.

'So what happened?' Ben asks.

It tore itself apart. Karma being karma, Alvarado became a crack addict and ended up in prison. A violent power struggle to fill the gap ensued and then gained a momentum of its own, with blood vendetta on top of blood vendetta. The *plazas* split into factions of a civil war, just as cocaine consumption drastically declined in the U.S. and the *plazas* found themselves fighting over a smaller pie.

And the Baja Cartel was taken over by Alvarado's nephews, the Lauter brothers, after they broke away from its original patron in the revolution. The AFs were very smart businessmen. Originally from Sinaloa, they came to Tijuana and infiltrated the cream of Baja society. Basically, they seduced a group known as the Juniors, the sons of doctors, lawyers, and Indian *jefes,* and gave them opportunities as drug smugglers. They also came across into San Diego and recruited the local Mexican gangs as enforcers.

From the mid to late nineties, the Lauters and the Baja Cartel *were* the Mexican drug trade. They co-opted the president's office itself, they had control over the Baja State Police and the local *federales,* they probably assassinated a Mexican presidential candidate and certainly gunned down a Catholic cardinal who publicly protested the drug trade, and got away with it.

Pride cometh before a fall. They pushed it too far. DC leaned all over the Mexicans to go after the Baja Cartel. Their patron, Benjamin, is now in the federal lockup in Dago; their chief enforcer, his brother Ramon, was gunned down in Puerto Vallarta by Mexican police.

Since then, it's been chaos.

Where once you had three *plazas* – 'cartel' is a rough equivalent – now you have at least seven fighting for dominance. The Baja Cartel itself, after pretty much a free-for-all, seems to have devolved into two rival factions:

'El Azul,' a former Lauter lieutenant, is backed by the Sinaloa Cartel, probably now the most powerful cartel. El Azul, thusly glossed because of his deep blue eyes, is a particularly charming guy who likes to drown his enemies in barrels of acid.

The remnants of the Lauter family, run by a nephew, Hernan, are allied with a group called Los Zetas, originally an elite counter-narcotics squad that went to the dark side and now work as enforcers for the Baja Cartel. Their particular party trip is lopping people's heads off.

'We saw the video,' Ben says.

'Hence your presence here today,' Dennis says. 'You want my advice, boys? And girl? I'll miss you, I'll miss your money, but run.'

Run far and fast.

51

Ben wants peace.

Give peace a chance, imagine there's no countries. Yeah, imagine there's no Mark David Chapman, either, see what that gets you. But it's Ben's business so they get out the lappie and find the return e-address on the Seven Dwarfs video.

Eighteen e-mails later they've set a meeting with the BC for the next day at the Montage.

Ben reserves a 2K-a-day suite.

When that's done, O smiles at her boys and asks, 'Can we go out? The three of us? *Really* go out?'

They know what she means by 'really.' The 'really' means do it right – get dressed up, hit the best places, drop a bundle, paint the town, do it.

We can go out is the answer.

Why not go out the night we *go* out? Ben thinks. Do it right. Celebrate the end of a successful business that's been good to us.

Embrace the change.

'Tomorrow night,' Ben says. 'Dress up.'

'I'll have to go shopping,' O answers.

52

When O gets home, Eleanor is pulling out of the driveway again.

Seems like that chick is always pulling *out* of driveways.

When O goes into the house, Paqu sits her down in the living room for a

Serious Talk.

'Darling girl,' she says, 'we need to have a serious talk.'

Which for O is like

Uh-oh.

'Are you breaking up with me?' she asks, sitting on the sofa cushion where Paqu has patted her hand to indicate that she should sit.

Paqu doesn't get it. She leans closer to O, her eyes get all soft and misty, she takes a deep breath and says, 'Darling, I need to tell you that Steve and I have decided to pursue our separate destinies.'

'Who's Steve?'

Paqu takes O's hand and squeezes it. 'Now, this doesn't mean that we don't love you. We do – very much. This has nothing to do with you and . . . it is *not . . . your . . . fault . . .* you do understand that, don't you?'

'Oh God, is he the pool guy?'

O likes the pool guy.

'And Steve is going to stay in town, you can see him anytime you want, this won't change your relationship.'

'Are we talking about *Six*?'

Paqu blinks. 'Steven – your stepfather?'

'If you say so.'

'We tried to make it work,' Paqu says, 'but he was so unsupportive of my life coaching and Eleanor said that I shouldn't be with a man who isn't supportive of my goals.'

'Six is unsupportive of your life coach coaching you to leave him,' O says. 'What an asshole.'

'He's a very nice man, it's just that—'

'Is this an *L Word* thing, Mom? Because Eleanor strikes me as a little—'

Dykey.

Not that there's anything wrong with that, O thinks. She and Ash have done some quasi-lesbo things under the influence of grass, X, and each other, but it really isn't their permanent thing, just sort of an emergency measure like Popsicles when you really want ice cream but the store is closed and that's all that's in the freezer.

Or maybe it's the other way around, metaphorically speaking.

She tries to imagine Paqu going down, strapping on a tool belt, or being femme to Eleanor's butch, but the image is scoop-your-own-eyes-out-with-a-grapefruit-spoon creepy and twenty-thousand-hours-in-therapy-and-you're-still-messed-up wrong so she gives it up.

85

As Paqu gently intones, 'So Steve is moving out.'
'Can I have his room?'

53

Lado drives home listening to some radio talk-show host go on and on about a 'wise Latina' and he thinks it's pretty funny.

He knows what a 'wise Latina' is: a 'wise Latina' is a woman who knows to shut her mouth before she gets the *back* of the hand, too, that's what a 'wise Latina' is.

His wife is a wise Latina.

Lado and Delores have been married for coming on twenty-five years, so don't tell him it don't work. She keeps a nice home, she's raised three beautiful, respectful kids, and she does her duty in the bedroom when requested and otherwise doesn't make demands.

They have a nice home at the end of a cul-de-sac in Mission Viejo. A typical suburban California home in a typical suburb, and when they moved up from Mexico eight years ago Delores was delighted.

Good schools for the kids, parks, playgrounds, excellent Little League program in which their two sons are stars – Francisco is a pitcher, Junior is an outfielder with a strong bat – and their oldest, Angela, made cheerleader at the high school this year.

It's a good life.

Lado pulls in to the driveway and turns off the radio.

Health care, who gives a shit about health care? You put money aside and you take care of yourself if you get sick. He had to set up a group insurance plan for his employees at the landscaping business and it pissed him off.

Delores is in the kitchen fixing dinner—

—wise Latina—

—when he comes in and sits down.

'Where are the kids?'

'Angela is at cheer practice,' Delores says, 'the boys are at baseball.'

She's still a *guapa*, Delores, even after three kids. Should be, he thinks, with the time she puts in at the gym. I should have invested in 24-Hour Fitness, got some of it back. Either that or she's at the spa getting something worked on – her hair, her skin, her nails, something.

Sitting there yapping with her friends.

Bitching about their husbands.

He don't spend enough time at home, he don't spend enough time with the kids, he never takes me out anymore, he don't help around the house . . .

Yeah, maybe he's *busy*. Making money to pay for the house he don't spend enough time in, *paying* for the cheerleader outfits, the baseball equipment, the English tutors, the cars, the pool cleaners, the gym, the spa . . .

She wipes the counter down in front of him.

'What?' he asks.

'Nothing.'

'Get me a beer.'

She reaches into the refrigerator

—new, three thousand dollars

grabs a bottle of Corona and sets it down – a little hard – on the counter.

'What, you unhappy again?' Lado asks.

'No.'

She sees a 'therapist' once a week. More money that she resents him busting his ass for.

Says she's depressed.

Lado gets up, steps behind her, and wraps his arms around her waist. 'Maybe I should make you pregnant again.'

'*Sí*, that's what I need.'

She slips from his grasp, walks over to the oven, and takes out a casserole of enchiladas.

'Smells good.'

'I'm glad you like it.'

'Kids home for dinner?'

'The boys. Angela's out with her friends.'

'I don't like that.'

'Good. You tell her.'

'We should sit down the whole family,' Lado says.

Delores feels like she's going to explode.

Sit down as a family – when you show up, when you drop in from God knows what you're doing, when you're not out with your *muchachos*, or doing your *putanas*, we should sit down the whole family. But she says, 'She's going to Cheesecake Factory

88

with Heather, Brittany, and Teresa. *Dios mio,* Miguel, she's fifteen.'

'Back in Mexico—'

'We're not in Mexico,' she says. 'We're in California. Your daughter is an American. That was the idea, wasn't it?'

'We should go back more often.'

'We can go next weekend, if you want,' she says. 'See your mother . . .'

'Maybe.'

She looks at a calendar fastened to the refrigerator by a magnet. 'No, Francisco has a tournament.'

'Saturday or Sunday?'

'Both, if they win.'

This is her life – professional chauffeur Baseball games, soccer matches, gymnastics, cheerleading, playdates, the mall, Sylvan Learning Center, dry cleaner's, supermarket, he doesn't even know.

Delores can't wait for Angela to get her license, drive herself anyway, maybe help with the boys. She's gained five pounds, all of it around the hips, just driving around sitting on her ass.

She knows she's still a good-looking woman. She hasn't let herself go like a lot of the Mexican wives her age do. All the time at the gym – Jazzercise, treadmill, weights, torture sessions with Troy – staying away from the sodas, the bread. The hours at the spa and the salon, getting her hair colored, her nails done, her skin so it's nice, and does he even notice?

Maybe they go out once a month as a family –
to TGIF's or Marie Callender's, California Pizza
Kitchen if he's feeling generous, but just the two
of them? To someplace nice? An adult restaurant
for a little wine, a nice menu? She can't remember
the last time.

Or the last time he fucked her.

As if he wanted to, anyway.

What's it been? A month? More? The last time
he came in at two in the morning a little drunk
and wanted some? Probably because he couldn't
find a whore that night, so I would have to do as
a *segundera*?

The boys come rolling in and they're all over
him. The pitches they made, the hits they got,
don't even bother to take their cleats off until she
yells at them to do it. Mud all over the kitchen
floor and tomorrow Lupe will bitch about the
extra work, the lazy Guatemalan *puta*. Delores
loves her boys more than life, but *dios mio* . . .

It hits her like a smack in the face

That she wants a divorce.

54

The Montage.

Resort Hotel.

Useta be a trailer park called Treasure Island.

Aaarggh, Jim, I know where the treasure be.

The treasure be in a luxury beachfront hotel
where the beautiful people will drop four thousand

a night for a suite. This in contrast to a bunch of retirees and trailer park trash living the SoCal sweet life (the *lo-cal sweet life?*) on the budget plan. Only money they're gonna make is for the owners of 7-Eleven, the liquor store, and the taco joint. Cheap chump change.

Plow that dump under and build a luxury hotel, give it a vaguely French name, figure out the most outrageous price you can get away with and then double it. If you build it they will come.

Ben and Chon check in to the suite but don't plan to spend the night. They slap down the 2K for the afternoon. Get a detached cabana with floor-to-ceiling view of the best right break in California. Have lunch catered by room service. Set up early so as not to disturb the meeting. The cartel reps don't like waiters walking in and out, figure they're really DEA agents all wired up.

No worries.

Ben brought in his own geeks, Jeff and Craig, two stoners who do all his IT. They have an office on Brooks Street they're never in. You want to find these boys you walk across the PCH down

Brooks to the bench overlooking the break and wave your arms. If they recognize you, they might paddle in. They do this because they can – they invented the targeting system for the B-1 bomber and now they make sure all of Ben's communications are sacrosanct.

How Jeff and Craig got the gig was, they

approached Ben at an outdoor table at Cafe Heidelberg downstairs from their 'office,' sat down at his table with their lattes and laptop, cranked the latter (not the latte) open, and showed him his last three days of e-mail.

Chon wanted to shoot them; Ben hired them.

On the spot.

Pays them in cash and herb.

So today they show up at the Montage and sweep the air, clear Ben's aura of any bad vibes from the alphabet agencies. Then they set up jammers so any eavesdropper is just going to get a sound like a junior high garage band playing with the feedback.

Chon does a sweep of another kind – walks the perimeter looking for potential shooters – *sicarios*, in Spanish. He knows it's an excess of cautious, over-due diligence, because no one's going to perpetrate any wet work at the Montage. Bad for business. Capitalists honor the First Commandment – Thou Shalt Not Fuck with the Money. You don't see no massacres on Rodeo Drive, either, and you ain't gonna – unless there's a post office nearby. So no one's likely to pump AK rounds into any golden geese here. It was still Treasure Island you could splatter chunks of flesh, bone fragments, and vital organs all over them single-wides and it's film-at-eleven, but it's the Montage now. The Montaaagge. It's French, it's genteel.

The rich do not mess with each other's money or leisure.

Or reluxation.

But Chon walks the beat because there's always that first time, in't it? Always that exception that proves the rule. That guy who says, 'Fuck it, the rules don't apply to me.' Above it all. The bozo who's going to go early John Woo all over the manicured lawns and flower beds just to show he doesn't give a fuck about convention.

Yeah, but we're talking about the Baja Cartel here, and they own a bunch of hotels in Cozumel, Puerto Vallarta, and Cabo, so they appreciate that flying lead makes the *touristas* nervous. No Germans are gonna go parasailing if they think a bullet is going to clip the line and send them floating away to the ozone. (God, that would *suck*, wouldn't it?)

Chon gets back from patrol, Ben twigs him about it. 'No guys with sombreros, big droopy mustaches, and bandoliers?'

'Fuck you.'

Which is how this thing began.

55

The two Cartel reps show up in gray Armani.

Black silk shirts open at the throat, but no gold chains.

French cuffs. Italian shoes.

In contrast to Ben – faded denim shirt, faded jeans, huaraches.

And Chon – black Rip Curl T-shirt, black jeans, Doc Martens.

Handshakes.

Intros around.

Ben.

Chon.

Jaime.

Alex.

Mucho gusto.

Jaime and Alex are your classic early-thirties, Tijuana-spawned, San Diego – born, dual-passport Baja aristocracy. Went to school in TJ until they were thirteen, then moved to La Jolla so they could attend the Bishop's School, then college in Guadalajara. Jaime is an accountant, Alex is a lawyer.

A&J aren't flunkies or errand boys.

They're highly valued, well-respected, handsomely compensated upper-middle management in the BC. They have stock options, medical benefits including primo dental, pension plans, and rotating use of the company condos in Cabo.

(Nobody ever quits the Baja Cartel. Not because of blood oaths or fear of getting clipped, but because . . . well, why would you?)

Ben serves lunch.

Wraps of duck in hoisin sauce with green onions. Club sandwiches with pancetta instead of bacon, smoked turkey, and arugula. Trays of sushi, platters of salad. Fresh fruit – mangoes, papayas, kiwi, pineapple. Pitchers of iced tea, Arnold Palmers, ice water. Gourmet cookies – chocolate chip, oatmeal raisin.

Coffee.

Very nice, very fresh.

Alex gets down to business.

'First of all,' he says, 'thank you for arranging this meeting.'

'Pleasure,' says Ben.

As if.

'We appreciate your willingness to dialogue,' Alex says.

'Dialogue' is a noun, not a verb, Chon thinks, annoyed. 'Decapitation' is also a noun, whereas 'beheading' could go either way.

'I can't help but wish,' Ben says, 'that you had extended an invitation to talk before you took certain actions.'

'Would you have responded?' Alex asks.

'We're always willing to talk.'

'Really?' Alex asks. 'Because the last time someone had a market dispute with you, I believe you settled it with a shotgun and very little, if any, conversation.'

He looks pointedly at Chon.

Chon looks back.

Fuck you.

'I can assure you,' Alex says, 'that we are not some motorcycle gang.'

'We know who you are,' Ben says.

Alex nods, then—

95

56

INT. MONTAGE SUITE – DAY

                    ALEX
We view Ben and Chon's as a prestige product –
a good cut above the norm – and we would
continue to market it that way. We're very
aware – and appreciative – of the fact that you
have a dedicated customer base with a prime
demographic, and the last thing we want to do
is disrupt that.

                    JAIME
Concur. Absolutely.

                    BEN
I'm glad to hear it.

                    ALEX
On the other hand—

                    CHON
Here it comes.

                    ALEX
—on the other hand, your sales structure – and I
think you'd admit this, Ben, if you were to be really
candid – is wasteful and inefficient. You're very

liberal in your compensation policies, your profit margin is nowhere near where it should be—

BEN

According to you.

ALEX

No, that's right, according to us, and we want to reorganize that to bring it up to where it can be.

JAIME

Maximize its full potential. Think 'greatest and highest use,' Ben.

BEN gets up, pours an iced tea, and walks around the room.

BEN

You're smart enough to realize that our retail customers – the high demographic that you value – are used to buying the product from the people that they're used to buying it from. It's more than just a business relationship. If you try to replace those people with . . .

CHON

A bunch of Mexican field hands.

BEN

. . . an anonymous sales force, it just won't work.

ALEX

That's where we're counting on you, Ben.

BEN

How so?

ALEX

To deliver your prime customer base along with
your fine product.

CUT TO:

57

'Our demand,' Alex says, 'is not that you stop
growing your product. Our demand is that you
sell your product to us at a price that allows us
to realize a reasonable profit. A big piece of
that puzzle is your continuing to produce the
product and helping to retain the customers who
purchase it.'

Jaime nods.

Apparently Alex got it right.

'So basically,' Ben says, 'you want us to come
work for you.'

'Effectively, yes.'

'No.'

'Why not?'

'Don't want to,' Ben says. 'I've always worked
for myself. I have no interest in working for anyone
else. Nothing personal, no offense.'

Alex says, 'I'm afraid our client will take it personally.'

Ben shrugs. Pop-psych-Buddhist truism – I can only control my actions, not other people's re-actions. Ben tries to explain. 'I want out of the dope business. I'm bored and it's become a drag. I want to do something different.'

'Such as?' Alex asks.

'Clean, renewable energy.'

Alex looks puzzled.

'Windmills and shit like that,' Jaime says.

'Oh.'

Alex looks puzzled.

'And solar,' Ben adds.

'Green,' Jaime says.

'There you go.'

'Couldn't you do both?' Alex asks.

'Again,' Ben answers, 'don't want to.'

He walks out, Chon behind him.

58

They look down at Aliso Creek Beach. The water is a deep, cold blue.

'You don't want to work for these guys, do you?' Ben asks.

'No,' Chon says. 'Let me rephrase that – fuck no.'

'Then we don't,' Ben says. 'I mean, they can't *force* us to grow herb.'

He appreciates the irony, though, that the Mexicans basically want to turn them into field

99

workers. Plant, grow, and harvest their crop for them. He digs the reverse colonialism of it, but it just isn't his thing.

Chon looks back at the suite. 'We could just kill them both. Get this party started.'

'Buddha would be so pissed.'

'That fat Jap.'

'Fat Indian.'

'I thought he was Japanese,' Chon says. 'Or Chinese. Some "ese."'

'Indianese.'

They walk back to the room.

59

Ben's fucking had it.

Reached the limits of his hydrocrisy.

Goes off on a rant:

Let's cut the shit, shall we? You guys are here at the behest of an organization that cut off seven people's heads, and you're talking like you're from Goldman Sachs? You represent a regime that murders and tortures and you sit here and lecture me about my business practices? You're going to increase profits by coercing me to sell at a low price – that's all, that's your genius 'business plan' – and now you want me to eat your shit and call it caviar? You can put a thug in an expensive suit and what you get is a well-dressed thug, so let's not pretend that this is anything other than what it is, extortion.

Nevertheless—

You want our marijuana business? You got it.

We can't fight you, don't want to fight you. We surrender.

Hasta la.

Vaya con.

AMF.

(Adios, motherfuckers.)

60

Alex turns to Chon. 'What do *you* have to say?'

Oh come on.

Come *onnnn.*

We *know* what Chon has to say.

We've covered that already.

61

It's the baditude.

His beatitude.

62

O is at—

South Coast Plaza.

The Mecca and Medina of SOC consumerism where retail pilgrims pay homage at a multitude of shrines:

Abercrombie & Fitch, Armani, Allen Schwartz and Allen Edmonds, Aldo shoes, Adriano

Goldschmied, American Eagle and American Express, Ann Taylor and Anne Fontaine

Baccarat, Bally, Balenciaga, Bang & Olufsen, Bank of America, Banana Republic (you can't make this shit up)

Bloomingdale's, Borders, Brooks Brothers, Brook*stone,* Bulgari

Caché, (speaking of which) Cartier, Céline, Chanel, Chloé, Christian Dior

Claim Jumper

De Beers, Del Taco (what the fuck is *that* doing in there), the Disney Store, DKNY, Dolce & Gabbana Emilio Pucci, Ermenegildo Zegna, Escada Façonnable, Fendi, Fossil, Fresh (no, seriously) Godiva, Gucci, Guess

Hermès, Hugo Boss

J.Crew, J. Jill, Jimmy Choo, Johnston & Murphy, Justice (uh-huh)

La Perla, Lacoste, Lalique, Limited (sans irony) Louis Vuitton

Macy's, McDonald's (see Taco, Del), Miu Miu (what the fuck?), Montblanc

New Balance, Nike, Nordstrom

Oilily, Optica, Origins, Oscar de la Renta

Piaget, Pioneer, Porsche Design, Prada, Pure Beauty (yup)

Quiksilver (surfing sells out; ambiguity intentional)

Ralph Lauren, Rangoni Firenze, Restoration Hardware, Rolex, Room and Board (again, without irony)

Saks, Salvatore Ferragamo, Sassoon, Sears (Sears?), Smith & Hawken, Sony, Sunglass Hut, Sur La Table, Swatch

Talbots, Teen Vogue, The Territory Ahead, Tiffany, Tinder Box (no shit, the fire *this* time)

Valentino, Van Cleef, Versace, Victoria's Secret, Victoria's Secret *Beauty*

Wahoo's Fish Taco (see 'surfing sells out'), Williams-Sonoma, Wolfgang Puck

Yves Saint Laurent

Zara

And a score of lesser saints.

63

O is one of the worshippers.

Would be a daily communicant if she had the cash. Did we say the girl loves to shop? Did we say that the girl maybe *lives* to shop? We're not slamming O; she'd tell you so herself.

'I shop,' she said to Ben one time after maxing out her card, 'because there is nothing else to do. I have no job, no serious interests, no purpose in life, really. So I buy stuff. It's something that I can do and it makes me feel better.'

'You're filling the internal void with external things,' Ben said.

(Sanctimonious Baddhist.)

'There you go,' O said. 'I don't adore myself, so I *adorn* myself.'

'You can't replace your absent father's love or

gain your suffocating mother's approval with material acquisitions,' Ben said.

(Annoying child of two psychotherapists.)

'That's what the *paid* shrink said,' O responded. 'But I can't seem to locate the Absent Father's Love and Suffocating Mother's *Approval Boutique*. Which one is it?'

'All of them,' Ben answered.

O changes therapists like some people change hairstyles. Well, like O changes hairstyles. And she's covered the whole fucking thing with all the shrinks – how Paqu feels guilty for not having provided her little girl with a stable home so tries to make up for it by supporting her and at the same time crippling her by enabling her blah blah; how Paqu is appalled by the idea of getting old and so has to keep her daughter a dependent child because having a truly adult daughter would mean that she is old blah blah blah, so—

'It's Paqu's fault,' O told Ben.

'It's Paqu's fault, *your* responsibility,' Ben answered.

(Patronizing moralist.)

He's tried. He's offered to set O up in her own small business, but O isn't interested in any business. He said he'd support her trying art, photography, music, acting, film, but O doesn't have a passion for any of that. He even invited her to join him overseas doing aid work, but—

'That's you, Ben. Not me.'

'It's immensely satisfying, if you can tolerate the absence of creature comforts.'

'I can't.'

'You could learn.'

'Maybe,' O said. 'How's the shopping in Darfur?'

'Shitty.'

'See . . .' O looked at her reflection in the store window. 'I'm the person a person like you should *hate*, Ben. But you don't because I'm so lovable. I have a great twisted sense of humor, I'm loyal like a dog, I have a cute face, small tits but I'm a freak in bed, and you're a loyal dog, too, B, so you love me.' Ben had no argument.

It was all accurate.

Another time, O did hit on something she could do. As a career.

'Cool,' Ben said. 'What?'

The freaking suspense killing him.

'Reality TV show star,' O said. 'I could have my own reality TV show.'

'What would the show be about?'

'Me,' O said, like, duh.

'Yeah, I know, but what would you *do* on the show?'

'Do,' like, as in a verb.

'The cameras just follow me around my day,' O said. 'Me being me. It would be like the Really Real Laguna Beach. A Girl Trying Not To Become A Real Housewife of Orange County.'

(O has more than once suggested they do a show

105

about her mother and friends, *The Real Cunts Of Orange Housewifies*.)

'But what do you do all day?' Ben asked. He knew, for one thing, that said camera crews wouldn't be complaining about early calls, anyway.

'You're a real buzzkill, Ben.'

Among other things, I do *you*, don't I.

'Okay, what's the show called?'

Again—

Duh—

O.

64

Now O whips out Paqu's black plastic and spanks it like a male dancer in a Madonna concert. Then she cruises over to José Eber and uses Mom's name to get an appointment for a cut, color, and styling. After that, it's off to the spa for a facial, then a redo on the makeup situation.

A One-Woman Stimulus Package.

65

Ben and Chon go to the volleyball nets at Main Beach, right by the old Hotel Laguna.

Figure it will feel good to bat the ball around a little. Alleviate their anger, clear their heads, help them decide what to do.

Your basic Fight v. Flight moment. Guess who goes for which?

'I say we send Alex and Jaime back in a cereal box,' says Chon, if you haven't guessed.

Set, spike, kill.

'I say we just go away for a while.'

Volley.

'Where can we go where they can't reach out?'

Volley.

'I know places.' Volley.

Ben does. There are dozens of villages in the remote Third World where they could hide and have a good time doing it, but what he really has in mind is this sweet little village on an Indonesian island called Sumbawa.

(Where they could be vewy vewy quiet.)

Clean beaches and green jungles.

Sweet people.

Chon says, 'You start running you never stop.'

Kill.

'Bad movie clichés notwithstanding,' Ben counters, 'running is fun and good for the cardiovascular system. You *should* never stop.'

Volley.

Chon isn't ready to give it up. 'There are some guys around from my old team. Some other guys I know. It would take some money . . .'

Volley.

'And only prolong the inevitable,' Ben says. 'They can't force us to do anything if we're not here and they can't find us. We go away for a while. By the time we're tired of traveling they'll probably have all killed each other off and we'll have a new set of people to deal with.'

Kill.

Chon leaves the ball in the sand.

Ben will never get it.

He thinks he's being Ben-evolent when in fact he's not doing enemies a favor, he's really hurting them. Because—

—lesson learned in I-Rock-and-Roll and Stanland—

66

If you let people believe that you're weak, sooner or later you're going to have to kill them.

67

The *patron* of the Baja Cartel agrees with Chon on this.

Except the *patron* of the BC is actually the *matron*.

68

When Elena Sanchez Lauter first took over leadership of the Baja Cartel, a lot of the men assumed that, being a woman, she was weak.

Most of those men are now dead.

She didn't want to kill them, but she had to, and for this she blames herself. Because she allowed the first man who disrespected her to get away with it. And the second, and the third. Rebellions, fighting, and internecine warfare broke out soon after. The other two cartels – Sinaloa and the Gulf – started to intrude on her territory. She blamed all of them for the burgeoning violence.

It was Miguel Arroyo, 'El Helado,' who set her straight.

Lado told her candidly, 'You have let people think that it's all right to defy you, that nothing will happen. *You* are therefore responsible for the bloodshed and the chaos. If you had displayed that first man's head on a stake, you would be feared and respected.'

She knew that he spoke the truth. She accepted her responsibility. 'But what do I do now?' she asked him.

'Send me.'

She did.

The story goes that Lado went straight to a bar in Tijuana owned by a *narcotraficante* called 'El Guapo.' Lado sat down at a table with his old buddy and drank half a beer before saying, 'What kind of men are we, we let a woman be in charge?'

'You, maybe,' El Guapo said. He looked around at the eight or so of his bodyguards. 'But that *puta* can suck my cock.'

109

Lado shot him in the stomach.

Before the shocked bodyguards could react ten men armed with machine guns came through the door.

The bodyguards dropped their guns to the floor.

Lado took a knife from his belt, leaned over the writhing El Guapo, pulled down his blood-soaked trousers, and asked, '*This* cock, *cabrón*?'

A swift swipe of the blade, then Lado asked the room, 'Anyone else want their cocks sucked?'

No one did.

Lado stuck it in El Guapo's mouth, paid for his beer, and left.

That's the story, anyway.

True, partly true, apocryphal, whatever – the point is that people believed it. What is recorded fact is that within the next two weeks seven more bodies were found with their genitals stuffed in their mouths.

And Elena got a new name.

Elena La Reina.

Queen Elena.

It's a shame, though, she thinks now, that—

Men teach you how they must be treated.

69

The bitch of it (yeah, yeah) is, she didn't want this.

Elena never wanted to head the cartel.

But as the only Lauter left standing it was her *duty*, her responsibility.

You want to see a busy woman, check out Elena Sanchez Lauter on the Day of the Dead, because she has to leave gifts on a lot of graves. A husband, two brothers, five nephews, uncounted cousins, friends beyond number, all killed in the Mexican drug wars.

Two other brothers in prison, one in Mexico, the other just over the border in a federal prison in San Diego.

The only male left was her then twenty-two-year-old son, Hernan, an engineer by training and profession, who would come to the throne by virtue of his mother's family name. Hernan was willing, in fact eager, to assume control, but Elena knew that he wasn't suited for it, didn't have the ambition, the ruthlessness – let's face it – the brains for the job.

Elena admits that he inherited his lack of character and intellect from his father, whom she had married at age nineteen because he was handsome and charming, and she wanted to get out of her parents' house and out from under her brothers' thumbs. She'd had a brief period living in San Diego, a tantalizing whiff of freedom, a truncated teenage rebellion that her family quickly sniffed (snuffed?) out before hauling her back to Tijuana, where the only escape was marriage.

And – face it – she wanted sex.

Which is the one thing at which Filipo Sanchez was competent.

He could make the rain fall for her.

Filipo knocked her up quickly, gave her Hernan, Claudia, and Magdalena, and got himself killed by carelessly and stupidly walking into an ambush. They sing songs about him now, beautiful *narco-corridos,* but Elena – if she was to be honest with herself – was almost relieved.

She was tired of his financial incompetence, his gambling, his other women, most of all his weakness. She misses him in bed, but nowhere else.

Hernan is his father's son.

Even if he managed to take the seat at the head of the table he would not be there for long before they killed him.

So she took the job instead, to save her son's life.

That was ten years ago.

And now they respect and fear her.

They don't think her weak, and, until recently, she didn't have to kill so many.

70

Elena has a lot of houses.

Right now she occupies the home in Rio Colonia, in Tijuana, but she also has three others in various parts of the city, a *finca* in the country near Tecate, a beach house south of Rosarito, another in Puerto Vallarta, a thirty-thousand-acre ranch in southern Baja, four condos in Cabo, and that's just Mexico. She owns another ranch in Costa Rica and two more houses on the Pacific side, an apartment in Zurich, another in Sète (she prefers Languedoc; Provence is too obvious), a flat in London she has stayed in exactly once.

Through shell corporations and DBAs she's purchased several properties in La Jolla, Del Mar, and Laguna Beach.

The Rio Colonia house is known as El Palacio. It's a compound, really, with outer walls and explosive-resistant gates. Squads of *sicarios* man the walls, patrol the grounds, and cruise the streets outside in armor-plated cars that bristle with guns. Other squads of gunmen guard the first set of gunmen against potential treason. The leaded windows now have grenade screens over them.

The 'master bedroom' is bigger than many Mexican homes.

She has furniture imported from Italy, a massive bed, a Renaissance-era mirror from Florence, and a flat-screen plasma television on which she secretively watches lurid soap operas. Her bathroom has a rain shower, a whirlpool bath, and magnifying mirrors that show every new line and wrinkle in what is still, at fifty-four, a pretty face.

In the U.S., Elena would be called a definite MILF.

She maintains her tight little body with rigid discipline in a private gym at the house and the *finca*. Men still sneak glances at her boobs; she knows she has a nice ass. But for what?

Elena's lonely in the big house.

Hernan, miserably married to a *bruja* of a harridan, has his own place now; Claudia is a new bride to a nice, dull factory manager; and then there's Magdalena.

Elena's wild child.

Her youngest, her baby, the unexpected.

Who seems to have intuited that her advent was unpredicted and responded by becoming unpredictable. It was as if Magda was always saying, through her actions, if you think I surprised you then, wait until you see what I have in store for you next.

A bright child who shocked with her miserable performance in school, and then, just when you had given up on her academic life ('Please, Maria, find her a patient husband'), she became a scholar. A talented dancer who decided that gymnastics were 'more her thing,' then quit abruptly to pursue horsemanship (as it were), then gave it up to return to the ballet. ('But I have *always* loved it, Mama.')

With her father's face and her mother's body, Magda broke a parade of boys on the wheel of her willfulness. Casually cruel, intentionally dismissive, a shameless tease – even her mother felt badly for a few of the tortured ('You will take it too far one day, Magda.' 'I have geldings harder to handle, Mama.') – Magda quickly

114

intimidated the pool of available suitors in Tijuana.

No matter, she wanted to leave.

There were student trips to Europe, summers with family friends in Argentina and Brazil, frequent outings up to L.A. to go to clubs and shop. And then just when Elena had become resigned to the fact that her baby was just a party girl . . . surprise – Magda returns from Peru with a serious desire to become an archaeologist. And Magda being Magda, there was not a college in Mexico that could satisfy her ambitions. No, it had to be the University of California, Berkeley or Irvine, although Elena was reasonably sure that her daughter threatened the faraway former to smooth the way for the relatively nearby latter.

Relatively close, yes, but Magda rarely makes the trip home. She's busy with her studies, and her video messages home show her in big eyeglasses, her hair pulled back into a plain pony-tail, her body hidden in formless sweaters. As if, Elena thinks, she fears her sexuality diminishes her intellect. Maybe she has the same concern about too-frequent visits home. So, except for holidays, Elena is left alone in her houses with only bodyguards, the soap operas, and her power for company.

It isn't enough.

It isn't what she wanted but it's what she has, and life has made her a realist. Still, she would like someone in her bed, someone at the breakfast table in the morning, someone to hold her, kiss her, make love to her. Sometimes she would like to open a window and yell out—

I'm not a monster

I'm not a bitch

(She knows they joke about her cock and balls, has heard the opposite punch line, 'When Elena gets her monthly, blood *really* flows.') I'm not—

Lady Macbeth

Lucrezia Borgia

Catherine the Great. I am

—a woman doing what she has to do. I am

—the woman you made me.

Elena is at war.

71

It's chaos now.

Where there used to be three cartels – Baja, Sonora, the Gulf – now there are at least seven, all fighting for turf.

And the Mexican government has launched a war on all of them.

Worse, she's faced with a rebellion in her own Baja Cartel. A faction has remained loyal to her and the old family name but another answers to El Azul, an enforcer who used to work for her brothers but would now be *patron*.

It has quickly evolved into open warfare. Baja averages five killings a day now. Bodies lie in the streets, or, as is El Azul's predilection, stuffed alive into barrels of acid. Elena has lost a dozen soldiers in the past month alone.

Of course, she has retaliated in kind.

And been smart – allying herself with the Zetas, formerly an elite antinarcotic police unit that went into business for itself as killers-for-hire. It was the Zetas who started the beheadings.

Killing people certainly causes fear, but decapitation seems to inspire a certain kind of primal terror. There's just something about the idea of having your head lopped off that really gets to people. Recently they had the idea of going to the IT people and getting it to go viral – old-school leadership technique meets modern marketing – and it has been an effective tool.

But the Zetas are expensive – cash on the barrelhead and their own drug turf as payment – so Elena has to acquire more territory just to stay even.

And El Azul has allies of his own.

The Sinaloa Cartel, perhaps now the most powerful in the country, adding money, soldiers, and political clout to Azul's rebellion. Putting yet more pressure on Elena to acquire more territory, make more money to hire more men, purchase more weapons, buy more political protection. Government officials have to be paid, police and army bribed . . . money, money, and always more money . . . so she has to expand.

But the only place left to go is north.

EL Norte.

Thank God she had the foresight to send Lado up there, what is it now, eight years ago? To quietly prepare the ground, recruit soldiers, infiltrate turf. So when she decided it was time for the Baja Cartel to take over the drug trade in California, Lado was established and ready.

Azul, of course, had followed suit – it was the obvious move – but so far Lado has him outmanned, outgunned, and outprepared up there.

It was Lado who decapitated the seven men.

Lado who will oversee the new marijuana market.

But now these two *Yanquis* want to play games?

She can't afford their foolishness. She's at war, she needs the income. It's a life-and-death matter for her

Don't let yourself think that they won't kill a woman. They have – she's seen the photos, the women with their mouths ducttaped, their hands tied behind their backs, always stripped, often raped first.

Men teach you how to treat them.

72

'"Fuck you"?' she asks now. 'He said that? In those words?'

Chinga te?

She talks to Alex and Jaime over the phone. 'I'm afraid so,' Alex says reluctantly.

'"Fuck you" ultimately means "Fuck me."'

118

Alex isn't going near that. He has a pretty *dulce* life going in California and he doesn't want to see it messed up with a drug war. They can keep that shit back in Mexico for all Alex cares. So he tries to make peace.

'They did agree to get out of the market immediately and totally,' he says.

Elena La Reina isn't buying. 'We didn't make them an offer to which we expected a counteroffer. We made a demand, with which we expected compliance. If we allow them to think that they can negotiate with us, sooner or later that will cause problems.'

'Still, if they are willing to abandon the field—'

'It sets a bad example,' Elena continues. 'If we let these two negotiate with us, talk to us like that, other entities will think that they are free to do the same.'

And she's concerned about these two Americans – the one, they tell him, is a smart, sophisticated, reasonable businessman, who has no stomach for bloodshed. The other is an uncouth, foul-mouthed barbarian who seems to relish violence.

In short, a savage.

73

Of course, most Americans are.

Savages.

And this is what most Americans don't understand – that most upper- to middle-crust

Mexicans think that Americans are uncivilized, unsophisticated, uncultured, rambunctious rustics who just got on a lucky streak back in the 1840s and rode it to steal half of Mexico.

Mexico is basically Europe laid over Aztec culture laid over Indian culture, but aristocratic Mexicans think of themselves as Europeans and the Americans as . . .

Well, Americans.

And the *Yanquis* can joke all they want about Mexican gardeners and field workers and illegal immigrants but what they don't get is that Mexicans think about those people as Indians and look down on them, too.

This is Mexico's dirty secret: the darker your skin, the lower your status. Which sort of reminds you of . . . of . . .

Uhhhh . . .

Anyway, lighter-skinned Mexicans look down their noses at darker-skinned Mexicans, but not as much as they look down on Americans.

(Black Americans? Fucking forget it.)

Yeah, okay, so Elena thinks that this 'Chon' is an *animale,* but a dangerous *animale.* The 'Ben' has his uses, but refuses to use them. In any case, she cannot brook their disobedience.

'So do you want them killed?' Alex asks.

Elena thinks it over and her answer is

Not yet.

74

Not yet.

Because a Dead Ben couldn't cultivate the excellent herb that produces so much potential profit. And a Live Ben would never do that if they kill his friend Chon. And this Chon, if past is prologue, has certain uses of his own.

So, wasteful to kill them.

Besides, it is better that these two be seen by the rest of the world to obey.

So—

INT. ELENA'S OFFICE – DAY

ELENA
What we need to do is force him to come work for us on our stated terms.

ALEX
How are we going to do that?

ELENA
(smiling cryptically)

I'll make him an offer he can't refuse.

75

Yeah, it's a goddamn shame that Elena is allergic to feline dander, because it would be great to have

121

a cat on her lap at that moment, but in reality she wouldn't fuck up an expensive dress with all that cat hair anyway.

But basically that's what she said.

Which begs a question

Doesn't it?

76

Elena knows that love makes you strong
And love makes you weak.
Love makes you vulnerable.
So if you have enemies
Take what they love.

77

O

looks fantastic in your basic little black dress that nevertheless must have cost a mortgage payment. Sheer black stockings and black fuck-me shoes. Her hair cut and dyed back to its 'natural' blonde, shiny and sleek.

'Wow.'

Ben says.

Chon nods his agreement.

She smiles at their approval, revels in it, basks in the sunshine of their admiration.

'You went all out,' Ben says.

'I did,' O answers. 'I'm going out with both my men.'

They take a limo to the Salt Creek Grille.

Hard to get a table there at short notice unless you're Ben the King of Hydro and then you could get a table at the freaking Last Supper if that's what you want. Yeah, they'd rush Jesus through dessert to accommodate Ben ('The gentleman at the end already took care of the bill, sir. With cash. Come back and see us again soon'), so table for three is *no problema.*

Beautiful there under the strings of lights on the PCH.

Nothing not to love.

Fine soft spring night, the air smells like flowers and O is beautiful, smiling, and happy. The food is great although Ben just has the miso soup, which he seasons with Lomotil tablets, the chemical cork, as any Third World sojourner knows.

Not O – she fired up some of Ben's appetizer boo and eats like a pregnant horse. Starts with the calamari then hits the French onion soup, the grilled ahi with cracked pepper crust and aioli, garlic mashed potatoes, Gujerati green beans, then the crème brûlée.

The wine flows.

No bill, no tab, no receipt but they leave a liberal 'as-if' tip, then go out to the limo, blaze up, and hit the exclusive hotel bars – the St Moritz, the Montage, the Ritz-Carlton, the Surf & Sand. Apple martinis and O grabbing glances everywhere, she's so hot with her two men.

'It's like that movie,' she says, standing on the patio of the Ritz looking out at the moonlight hitting the breakers.

'What movie?' Ben asks.

'That old movie,' O says, 'with Paul Newman when he was alive and Robert Redford when he was young. I was home sick one day from school and it was on cable.'

Butch Cassidy and the Sundance Kid,' Chon kicks in. 'If I follow O's drift, you're Butch and I'm Sundance.'

'Which one was Butch?' Ben asks.

'Newman,' Chon answers. 'Which fits, because you're into the philanthropist thing. I'm the sexy shooter.'

'I'm the girl in it,' O says happily.

'Didn't they get killed at the end?' Ben asks.

'Not the girl,' says O.

79

Lado gets tired
Following these rich spoiled *gueros* up and down the Gold Coast.

Them in their limo.

Good to get a look at them, though. The one moves like a killer and they'll have to be careful with him. This is the one that said 'Fuck you' to

Elena (and we already know how this kind of thing goes down with Lado).

The other looks soft and easy.

No problem.

The *puta, la guerita?*

What Lado can't figure out is, whose woman is she? Which cock does she suck? They both treat her like she's their woman – an arm around the shoulder a peck on the lips, but the men don't look like they're going to butt heads.

Could it be that she does them both?

And do they know?

And not care?

Fucking savages.

80

After the bar crawl they take a walk on the boardwalk at Main Beach.

Laguna.

A gentle arc anchored by the Inn at Laguna on the north and the old Hotel Laguna on the south. Tall graceful palm trees, tropical flowers, moon sparkling on the small waves. The basketball courts, the volleyball courts, the playground.

The old lifeguard tower.

One of Ben's favorite spots on earth and probably why he always eventually comes home.

So they walk, a little drunkenly, and talk about retirement from the dope business. What he and Chon are going to do, who they're going to be.

O is geeked by the energy idea, wonders if maybe there's a place for her and the answer is of course. This business is different from the last business, no risks legal or otherwise, all above board, transparent in the open air.

Launder the dope money, it comes out sunshiny clean as energy.

They're happy about this.

Even Chon is happy about this now he's thought a little and drank a lot. Might be nice to let the adrenaline level drop a little. Will take some getting used to, but it might be a good thing. Swap the hardware of guns for the hardware of turbines, blades, and panels. Shoot electricity around like streams of bullets.

Light it up.

Ben is happy.

Walking on this beach he loves with these people he loves. The arc of the coast wraps around him like their arms.

81

Elena lies in her big lonely bed and looks at a soap opera.

Watches other people's passion.

Magda calls from school.

How are you? I'm fine. How are you? Nothing new, really . . .

Elena knows that the call is meant to conceal more than it reveals but she understands and even

126

approves. Good for the girl to get out and have her own life. As much as she can, anyway, shadowed everywhere by bodyguards. She has told them to be discreet and that they are security, not spies – she does not need to know what she does not need to know.

The light from the television flickers on the grenade screen outside the window and Elena watches that for a few moments. Then the two lovers on the screen start to yell at each other and she turns her attention to that and the argument resolves in an embrace and a fiery kiss.

When the phone rings it's Lado.

The two *gueros* went out with a girl and they all went back to the same house.

'A whore?' Elena asks.

'Not a professional,' Lado answers. 'I don't think.'

She looks and acts like a rich girl.

Elena hears this and wonders about Magda. Does she look and act like a rich girl? Probably so. I should have a word with her about toning it down.

'Whose girlfriend is she?' Elena asks. 'Does she belong to Mr Let's Cut the Shit or Mr Fuck You?'

'I don't know,' Lado answers.

He explains his difficulty.

'You're there now,' she says.

'Outside the house, yes.'

'And the three of them are still there?'

'Yes.'

'Interesting.'

127

Not to Lado. He's bored. He has four good men with him, all *mujados*, paperless, untrackable, stone killers who could be back across the border before the sun goes up. The three *gueros* are drunk and stoned – this might be the easiest they would ever have it against the killer—

'I can do it now.'

'That means the girl, too, though.'

Lado lets his silence answer.

82

Another awkward uncharacteristic silence.

When they get back to Ben's.

O wondering what (who) to do.

But Ben busts out

The sex dope.

Moist, musky, earthy, tasty, fetid *fucking* boo.

One toke busts the dew out on your blossom, two makes you flow flow flow. You swell and flow, grip and let go, and cry. Tears from your pussy, tears from your eyes, your nips would weep if they could, it's that good. And that's for the women, for the men it's

Taproot time.

Could bust through a concrete sidewalk looking for the light, searching for sun. So hard, so hard so hard but you last, literally for fucking ever. Fucking forever, every nerve on your skin a shimmering pleasure center, like, she touches your freaking *ankle* you moan.

Ben & Chon's Sex Dope.

Responsible for more orgasms on the West Coast than Doctor Johnson.

No wonder the Mexicans want it.

Everybody wants it.

You give this to the Pope he'd be frisbeeing condoms off the balcony to grateful, adoring thousands. Telling them to go for it. God is good, get laid. God is love, get good.

O takes two tokes.

OMG.

O My fucking G.

Spot.

Chon hits on it, too. Takes one long one but one long one is long enough. O and Chon splayed out on the bed. He flops down beside O, who takes another whack and hands it to Ben. He sucks it down and this is more than a toke, it's a decision, an agreement, a tacit acceptance that they're going to cross a river.

They all feel it.

O, the center, the middle, the conduit of their tripartite love.

They're in no hurry, though, every slow move is fascifuckinating. Takes Chon about thirty-seven minutes just to peel the shoulder strap of her dress down her arm and she feels like she's going to come just from that. She has on this transparent black bra and he spends a good five years stroking her breast with the back of his fingers watching feeling that nipple trying to poke through the material like a plant coming up in the spring until she reaches behind and unsnaps the damn thing (Mr Gorbachev, take down this wall) because she wants to feel his skin on her breast before it just bursts open and when he does she has a little one right there and one when he puts his lips on her nip and the colors in the room get crazy.

Colors go positively psychotic when he slides down, opens her with his fingers, and tongues her. Very unlike Chon, this oral loving, he's usually a right-to-the-dicking guy but now he takes his time and hums little happy tunes into her (Little Miss Echo), presses his finger onto her spongy spot, and she writhes and wriggles and wiggles, pants and moans and coos and comes and comes and comes (O!) and then rolls to her side, yanks down his jeans, grabs his dick, and puts it inside of her (where it belongs).

Ben strokes her back. Runs his fingers slowly up and down her spine, along the curve of her ass, down the backs of her thighs, her calves, her ankles, her feet, and back up again.

Exquisite.

O says, 'I want both. Both my boys.'

She reaches behind her to feel his warm hard-soft wood. Ben is pine, no – oak, no – sandalwood, sweet, scented, sacred sandalwood and she places him where she wants him, Chon's cold-hot steel pumps her fills her but not all of her then she feels Ben push and there's this little resistance but then he's inside and now she has both her men inside her (where they belong).

Who knew they were such musicians, who knew they were a duet capable of this rhythm, this beat this dance? Who knew she was an instrument capable of these notes? A slow song at first, slow and soft, largo and piano, then the pace picks up, one strain comes on as the other recedes, back and forth, a relentless driving beat. Ben's hands on her breasts, Chon's on her waist, she touches Chon's face, Ben's hair. Her two men, driving in her, playing her, she hears herself scream now, no refuge from the pleasure, no break, no eighth-note rests, no respite, no sanctuary, one thin membrane separating them, she's dripping, swelling, grab- bing, gripping, pouring, shooting screaming one long note as they come together.
OOOOOOOOOOOOOOO

83

Elena can't sleep.
Thinking about the girl.

84

Chon on the difference between advertising and pornography:
Advertising gives beautiful names to ugly things.
Pornography gives ugly names to beautiful things.

Should be awkward (What did we *do* last night?!) in the morning but it isn't.

It's EZ.

Happy cool.

Chon rolls out first. Goes out on the deck and does his push-ups. Ben still sleepy-warm in the bed. He gets up a few minutes later, hears the shower running and O singing some tune off the radio.

They gather around the breakfast table.

Grapefruit, sliced mango, black coffee.

O smiling happily.

The boys quiet until Ben looks across the table at Chon, holds his thumb and index finger a millimeter apart, and says, 'We're *that* close to being gay.'

They laugh for half an hour.

Collective dicks.

86

On the radio some airwave jabber-jockey goes on and on about the new prez being a socialist while another mike-monkey 'defends' him.

A fight as real and choreographed as a WWF match. The liberal in one corner, the conservative in the other – pick your villain, pick your hero.

Ben likes the new POTUS because the cat

smoked weed, snorted crack, wrote about it, and got away with it.

Nobody said dick.

Not in the primaries, not in the campaign, not at all.

And you know why?

Because he was black.

And you have to love that.

No disrespect to Dr. King, Ben thinks, but the giddiest guy on Inauguration Day would have been Lenny Bruce.

Paqu was, like, *appalled* when Obama got elected.

Like, what's next, a Mexican?

At least the White House lawn will look good, O comforted her.

87

'I hope he *is* a socialist,' Ben says. 'Socialism works.'

Worked for Ben and Chonny's, certainly.

Chon doesn't believe in socialism
                or communism or capitalism.

The only 'ism' he believes in is
                jism.

O, the sacramental vessel of his faith,
                laughs.

'What about hedonism?' Ben asks, just enjoying the game because Chon is one of the least hedonistic people he knows. Chon likes his pleasure, no doubt, but he is also a disciplined daily self-torturer who runs miles of beach, swims miles of ocean, does a thousand push-ups and pull-ups and sit-ups and bangs his bare fist into a wooden post until it bleeds (the fist, not the post).

'Nope, not hedonism,' Chon answers. 'In my world, there's only

         he do or he don't ism

because when it comes down to a man getting it done, either

         he do, or he don't.'

O concurs.

Happy she has two he do's.

'No, I've got it,' Ben says. 'Nihilism.'

'Nihilism,' Chon says. 'Now you might be onto something.'

Okay, that's pretty funny, O thinks.

88

Then Ben sez—

'I think we should go on a little trip.'

He and Chon looking all conspirational. For two dope dealers, O thinks, they are amazingly transparent. She should have them teach her to play poker with them, take everything they own.

'We?' O asks. Like who is the we in 'we'? The two of us – in which case, which us – or we three (kings of Orient are)?

'The three of us,' Ben clarifies. 'New life, new beginning.'

'Are we going to Bolivia?' O asks.

'I'm thinking Indo.'

He knows this pretty little village on the ocean. The people are beautiful and friendly. Ben has put a clinic, a school, and a water treatment plant in this village. He has brought in cosmetic surgeons to heal children. The men of the village – small, slight men who wear skirts – carry long, curved blades and love Ben.

'Indo?' she asks.

'Indo,' Ben says.

'I'll have to do more shopping.'

'Buy cool stuff.'

'I *always* buy cool stuff.'

'No, I mean *cool* stuff. For hot, humid weather,' Ben says.

'And is your passport up to date?'

'I think so.'

She thinks so because Paqu keeps her passport in a desk drawer so that O doesn't fuck up and lose it.

Or go someplace.

'Go get your passport, buy some cool clothes, meet us back here at five.'

'Coolie cool.'

89

When O asks Paqu how things with Eleanor are, Paqu gives her an odd, uncomprehending look.

'Eleanor?' O prompts. 'Your life coach?'

135

'Jesus is my life coach now.'

Uh-oh.

Turns out Paqu has joined a megachurch up in Lake Forest. Paqu being Paqu, of course it's the largest church in the nation.

'Uhhh, do you know anything about Jesus's life, Mom?' O asks. 'Read a biography or anything?'

'Yes, darling, the Bible.'

'Have you gotten to the end, because—'

'I've accepted Christ as my personal savior.'

'—it didn't turn out that well for the guy. You know, the crucifixion thing and stuff.'

Three Things I Will Do Today to Get Myself Nailed to a Cross:

1. Piss off the money changers
2. Piss off the Romans
3. Tell my dad I don't want to

(Young Jesus hangs from a cross, learning a lesson about trust. 'Just get up there, I'll catch you.')

'Would you pray with me, Ophelia?' Paqu asks.

'Yeah, no. Thanks, though.'

'I'll pray for you.'

'Where's my passport?'

This sets off Paqu's alarm system. 'Why?'

'I want it.'

'Are you going somewhere?'

'I'm thinking France.'

'What's in France?'

'I dunno, French stuff. The French.'

'Is it a French *man,* Ophelia?' Her skin is stretched so tight across her bones you could drum on it.

O is tempted to say that actually she got double-teamed by two perfectly fine all-American guys last night, just to see her face actually go jigsaw puzzle, but she doesn't. She wants to say that she's going to Indo with these two men and maybe try to build some kind of *life,* she wants to say goodbye, but she doesn't say that, either.

'It's *my* passport,' she hears herself whine.

'In the upper left desk drawer in my office,' Paqu says. 'But we need to talk about this.'

Yeah, we need to talk about a lot, Mom, O thinks. But we won't. She goes into Paqu's office, digs around in the desk drawer, finds her passport, and goes out the back door.

B4N.

90

Ben and Chon get busy.

Lots to do, disengaging.

First they get on the phone, the text, e-mail to all their retailers and tell them to take a vacay, go off the radar for a spell. Lots of bitching, push-back, and questions, but Ben is firm about it.

Trading has been suspended.

Just giving you a heads up.

Heh.

Then he and Chon drive down to Cafe

Heidelberg on the PCH and Brooks Street to have coffee and a pastry with Ben's money guy. They have to pass three Starbucks to get there but Ben won't go in the joints. He will only buy 'fair trade' coffee. Chon has a different idea about what fair trade means. He gives them money, they give him coffee, that's fair trade. Anyway, he doesn't care, the Heidelberg is just fine.

He makes Ben drive even though Ben is a shitty driver. But Chon wants his hands free for the Glock on his lap, the shotgun on the floor, and the Ka-Bar in his belt just in case they run into a deer that needs leveling or if things get up close and personal.

Ben thinks the arsenal is excessive.

'It's a business negotiation,' he says.

'You saw the video,' Chon answers.

'That was Mexico,' Ben says. 'This is Laguna Beach. The cops wear shorts and ride bicycles.'

'It's too civilized here?'

'Something like that.'

'Uh-huh. Then why are we going to Indonesia?'

'Because there's no point in being careless.'

'Exactly.'

They find a parking spot on Brooks, and Ben fills the meter with quarters. For some reason, Ben always has quarters. Chon never has quarters.

Spin Dry is already at a table outside.

Spin D used to be an investment banker with an established bank in Newport Beach. Then he

138

discovered Ben's product, and that he could make more money laundering Ben's profits. The bank was not unhappy to see him go.

Now Spin spends the early-morning hours monitoring the money markets in Asia and the Pacific, and the rest of the time riding his bike, going to the gym, and banging Orange County Trophy Wives who get their Mercedes and jewelry from their hubbies and their cookies from Spin.

Spin is a happy man.

He rode his bike here and he's dressed in one of those stupid skintight Italian bodysuits with the matching cap.

Chon thinks he looks like an idiot.

'S'up?' Spin asks, because he thinks talking like a surfer who's been hit in the head too many times will make him not forty-three.

'Not us,' Ben says. 'I need to go off the grid for a while.'

Spin wipes the cappuccino foam off his upper lip. 'S'cool.'

'Yeah, it's not, really,' Ben says. 'But it's where we're at. I need you to set up a new line for me, double-blind, liquidate five hundred K, and I want everything else washed fresh. Whole new cycle, make it go away somewhere for a while.'

'No worries.'

No worries – every time Chon hears 'no worries' he worries.

'I want to pick it up clean in Jakarta,' Ben tells Spin. 'Half in dollars, half in local currency.'

'Lot of lettuce to be carrying around, boss.'

'It's okay,' Ben says. 'Also, so you can plan your personal finances, I want to tell you that we're getting out of the old *pista secreta*.'

'*Amigo* . . .' Spin is shocked.

A world without Ben and Chonny's?

'We've had a good run,' Chon says. 'You've made a lot of money.'

A lot is a lot.

But never enough.

91

O decides to start at Banana Republic.

In South Coast Plaza, natch.

(Don't geek, we're not going to go through the whole list again.) She never sees the car that followed her home, follows her out again. She parks the car and goes in.

Esteban, one of the three men in the car following her, calls Lado.

92

Who is in his office dealing with landscaping shit.

Everybody wants everything done at the same time – which is right now – and they want the same service for less money. They're all looking for bargains these days, the ones who haven't just dropped the service – a comical sight, a *guero* trying to start a weed whacker – but Lado hasn't been hit too hard. Most of his business is condo associations and he's also found a little recession niche market – banks and Realtors need fore-closed properties cleaned up in order to sell them.

He sees the caller ID and walks outside to take the call.

Gives the Nike response –Just Do It.

These boys are good, they know what to do.

93

O decided to go all Kristin Scott Thomas with the travel wardrobe.

Spare but sensual.

Lotsa white and khaki. What she can't find is *that* hat – big, floppy, packable, but still sexy – so she decides to leave SCP and drive over to Fashion Island in Newport Beach.

She gets back in her car, turns the key, and feels the blade at the back of her neck.

'Just drive, *chica*.'

She drives where the voice tells her, across Bristol into Costa Mesa, down some streets and to the back side of a little strip mall, where a Mexican in a baseball cap gets in the passenger side and jabs a needle in her thigh.

94

Chon gets the e-mail with the attached vid-clip.
Calls Ben over.

It's O.
Sitting in a chair in a nondescript room.
Ugly yellow walls.
A chain saw at her feet.

95

Then the vid artist does this really cute thing —
O's head just pops off her shoulders and starts
floating around the screen.
A phone number comes up.

96

Ben hits the number.
Asks, 'What do you want?'
Chon says, 'Give me the phone.'
Ben isn't doing that. For Chon to say, 'Fuck
you,' and then they *really* separate O's head from
her body.
Reality versus virtuality.
'I need proof of life,' Ben says.
A phrase he remembers from some movie.
No problem
Skype.

97

O looks scared.
Of course she does.
Scared and stoned. They gave her something.

'Hi.'

'Hi.'

'Did they hurt you?' Chon asks.

Ready to *rip*.

O says, 'No, I'm okay.'

Ben says, 'I'm so sorry about this.'

'It's okay.'

Her image goes off the screen. Replaced by audio.

98

An electronically altered voice says, 'Let me speak with Mr Let's Cut the Shit.'

'I'm here.'

'Let's cut the shit, shall we? You will make the first delivery to me, at the price I demand, within the next five hours or you will receive an e-mail that you will not like.'

'No problem.'

'Really? Because it was a problem before.'

'It's not now.'

'Good. Now let me speak to Mr Fuck You.'

'I'm on,' Chon says.

'You insulted me.'

'I'm sorry.'

'Sorry isn't good enough.'

'Whatever you want,' Chon says.

'I assume you have a pistol. Get it.'

Chon gets his .38. 'I have it.'

'Stand in front of the camera where I can see you.'

Chon does.

'Now stick it in that big mouth of yours,' the voice says.

They can hear O scream, 'Chon, donnnn't!!!'

But they also hear a chain saw start up and the voice say, 'Her hands first . . .'

'I'm doing it, I'm doing it!'

Ben's in shock. Weird, sick, nightmare shock.

Chon opens his mouth and swallows the barrel.

'Now pull the trigger.'

Chon squeezes the trigger.

99

'Stop!'

'Jesus Christ.' Ben's knees give out from under him and he's suddenly sitting on the floor with his face in his hands.

'Take the gun out.'

Chon slowly pulls the barrel from his mouth. Slowly because he feels like he's moving under-water, and also because he doesn't want to fuck up and shoot himself taking the gun *out* of his mouth.

'The next time that I ask you to do something, I assume that I will not hear "Fuck you"?'

Chon nods.

'Good. There is a man in San Diego who is giving me a problem. You will be called with details. If I don't hear about his death within five hours, I will kill your friend. *Buenos dias.*'

Audio goes dead.
Screen goes blank.

100

What to do, what to do?
Go to the FBI?
The DEA?
Ben is perfectly willing to do that, even though
it would doubtless mean years in prison for him,
if that would save O. But it wouldn't – it would
only kill her. If the feds could handle the cartels,
they would have shut them down already.
So that's out.
Their other alternative is . . .
Nada.
They're fucked.
This is Ben's mistake, and it goes back a long
way. Ben always figured that he could live with a
foot in two worlds. One Birkenstock in the offi-
cially criminal marijuana-dealing demimonde and
the other in the world of civilization and law.
Now he knows that he can't.
He has both feet stuck in the jungle.
Chon never harbored such illusions.
Chon has always known that there are two
worlds:
The savage
The less savage.
The savage is the world of pure raw power,
survival of the fittest, drug cartels and death

squads, dictators and strongmen, terrorist attacks, gang wars, tribal hatreds, mass murder, mass rape.

The less savage is the world of pure civilized power, governments and armies, multinationals and banks, oil companies, shock-and-awe, death-from-the-sky, genocide, mass economic rape.

And Chon knows—

They're the same world.

'What are we going to do?' Ben asks.

'As soon as the intel comes in,' Chon says, 'I'm going to hop in my car and kill whoever they ask me to. You're going to get your ass off the floor and deliver the dope.'

'You're going to kill someone for him?!'

'I did it for Cheney and the Sock Puppet,' Chon says. 'What's the diff?'

The phone rings.

Chon grabs it.

'Yeah . . . yeah . . . got it.'

'They gave you the address?' Ben asks.

'Sort of.'

'What do you mean, sort of?'

'It's a freaking boat,' Chon says.

It's a freaking boat—

—at last, at last, putting Chon's SEAL training to use.

101

This Chon is a very brave man, Elena thinks. And he must love this girl very much.

146

It makes her a little sad, nostalgic for passion.
But now she knows what she wanted to know—
These men will do anything – anything – for this woman.
It is their strength and their weakness.

102

O looks up at Lado's black eyes.
He looks at his watch.
Says nothing.
It's good O doesn't know what he's thinking, doesn't have access to this particular interior monologue:
Five hours, *segundera,* and you're mine. Whore that sleeps with two men, maybe I rip you up before I cut you up, *guerita.* You're small, a spinner what they call it. I would tear you up, you won't need two men, just one real man.
Five hours, *putana.* Me, I hope they don't make it.
Yeah, O can't hear that stream-of-consciousness gurgling.
Good thing –even through the Oxy she's terrified, then—
Lado mimes pulling the starter cord of a chain saw.
Makes a noise—
Rum rum ruuuummmm . . .

103

Chon divides the world into two categories of people:

Him, Ben, and O

Everybody Else.

He'd do anything for Ben and O.

For Ben and O he'd do anything to Everybody Else.

It's just that simple.

104

Chon screws the silencer onto the pistol

Puts it into the wetbag

Zips the bag up tight.

Beyond the harbor the lights of the San Diego skyline reflect on the smooth black bay.

A layer of color painted on the water.

A Photoshop trick.

Life imitating (graphic) art.

Chon blackens his face, ties the bag's lanyard to his wrist, and checks the Ka-Bar strapped to his right leg.

Lowers himself into the water.

Soundlessly.

MOS.

It's a short distance to the boat but he has to do most of it underwater so as not to be seen as he passes the other sailboats moored in the harbor. All the training the navy paid for and put him through and didn't use he uses now.

Glides just under the surface, makes barely a ripple.

A water snake.

A sea otter.

He comes up twice to check his position, see the boat's mooring lamps.

Behind curtains, a light on in the cabin.

Twenty yards from the boat he angles to the left, toward the aft. Swims to the ladder and holds on to a rung as he opens the bag and takes out the pistol.

One clip – nine rounds.

Nine oughta do it.

He climbs on board.

105

They give O more OxyContin.

They don't have to force it down her throat, either, she's glad to take it.

Because she's fucking terrified, right?

She doesn't know where she is, she doesn't know what they're going to do with her, she has images of floating heads floating around her head.

You sit on a bed in a small locked room for hours and hours with nothing to do but imagine someone putting a chain saw to your neck, you'd take as many sedatives as they want to give you.

You just want to go to sleep.

When O was little she'd lie on her bed in her room listening to Paqu and One screech at each other and all she'd want to do was sleep to stop the sounds. She'd pull her knees up, stick her hands between her legs, shut her eyes tight.

Asking herself

Am I Sleeping Beauty

Will my Prince(s) Charming come wake me?

106

Chon opens the cabin door.

With his left hand.

Gun in his right.

The problem is out cold.

With a woman beside him.

Very pretty. Honey hair splayed on the pillow, naked shoulders above the sheet, full, kiss-swollen lips slightly open. Chon hears her breathing.

She's the lighter sleeper. Opens her eyes and then sits up and looks at Chon incredulously. Is he a dream? A nightmare? No, he's real, but who is he? A burglar? On a boat?

She sees the gun, knows how the man asleep beside her has the money for the boat and her honey hair. Looks at Chon and murmurs, 'No. Please. No.'

Chon shoots twice.

Into his head.

Problem solved.

Swallowing a scream, she jumps out of the bed, lunges into the head, slams and locks the door behind her.

Chon knows what he needs to do.

Back in the water.
Under the water.
Powerful strokes propelling him
Chon cuts through the blackness
Swimming strong and fast
For an O-lympic gold medal.
Where he knows the water is deep he drops the
gun and lets it sink to the murky bottom.
He knows it was a mistake
Not killing the woman, but—
he thinks, as he plunges up through the painted
water—
I'm not a savage.

I couldn't have done it.
A mantra Ben involuntarily repeats, his mind on
continuous loop as he races to the grow house.
I couldn't have done it.
Couldn't have pulled the trigger on myself, even
to save O.
Would have wanted to.
Would have tried to, but—
I couldn't have done it.
With the mantra comes shame, and, surprisingly
for the product of two shrinks, a derogation of his
manhood.
You feel less a man for not blowing your own

brains out? On command? Ben asks himself. As if you've ever equated masculinity with machismo. That's crazy. That's beyond crazy, that's over the crazy horizon.

Yeah, but crazy is where we live now.

The Republic of Crazy.

And Chon would have done it.

Check that – Chon did it.

And what if

what if

what if

they had ordered Chon to shoot not himself but Me.

He would have done it.

Sorry, Ben. But *bam*.

And he would have been right.

Ben pulls off onto the cul-de-sac in the quiet suburban neighborhood in the eastern reaches of Mission Viejo. The 'Old Mission.' (Meet the new mission, same as the old mission.) The house is at the top of the circle, its manicured backyard separated by a wall from a long slope of chaparral that shelters rabbits and coyotes.

He pulls in to the driveway, gets out, walks up, and rings the bell.

Knows a surveillance camera is on him.

(Better be, anyway.)

So Eric knows it's him when he comes to the door.

Eric doesn't look like a dope farmer, he looks like an actuary. Short light-brown hair, receding on his forehead, horn-rimmed glasses. All dude needs is a pocket protector to be totally dweeb.

'Hi.'

'Hi.'

He walks Ben through the living room – sectional sofa, La-Z-Boy recliner, big-screen TV playing *America's Got Talent* – and then the kitchen – granite countertops, oak island, stainless-steel sink – to the indoor swimming pool under its canopy of tinted Plexiglas.

There's a fucking pool, all right.

With grow lamps, drip lines.

Metal halide – vegetative phase

High pressure sodium – flowering phase

A fecund hothouse.

Ben looks at his watch.

Motherfucker.

Realizes that his armpits are soaked with anxiety sweat.

'It's all packed up?' he asks.

'Everything that's harvest-ready.'

'Let's get it loaded.'

A soccer-mom van, stripped of the backseats, waits out back. Ben and Eric load the kilos in, then Ben gets behind the wheel and starts the motor.

He has forty-three minutes to get to Costa Mesa.

Slicing through SoCal
Cutting through a California night
The freeway (5) is soft and warm and
Welcoming
But for Ben
The green exit signs are like steps climbing up
a scaffold
Toward O.
Each one marking precious time, saying miles
to go – And miles to go before she sleeps
Aliso Viejo, Oso Parkway, El Toro
Lake Forest, Culver, MacArthur
John Wayne Airport now off to his left, glowing
in white light, shut down for the night now so that
takeoffs don't disturb the slumber of Orange
County—
Jamboree, because the Boy Scouts camped
there.
Ben does eighty-five with a vanload of dope.
Doesn't want to speed like that but has to because
the clock is running
Irvine Spectrum with its unlikely Ferris wheel
and
Irvine Amphitheater proclaiming on its marquee
the coming of Jimmy Buffett, o come, ye
Parrothead faithful . . .
Ben sees, from the corner of his eye
The CHP car parked in the median
Lying in ambush

Like death does

(Cancer, heart attacks, aneurisms, all waiting patiently in the median strip)

He prays that the cop has better things to do, replays a Springsteen song in his head ('Mister state trooper please don't stop me, please don't stop me, please don't stop me'), not because he fears the years in prison but because it would mean O's death and he glances in the rearview mirror to see if the cop pulls out (please don't stop me, please don't stop me), and he doesn't.

Ben fucking can't fucking breathe.

Hands soaked on the sweat-slick wheel.

Finally, Bristol Street.

South Coast Plaza.

O's hunting grounds.

He exits left on Fairview.

Head on a swivel, he looks for the address they gave him, street numbers matching a little strip mall.

Come on, come on, come on

Where is it, where is it, where is it

His stomach aching, cramping in tension, he feels like he might shit himself, then sees—

The wooden sign '33–38.'

A liquor store, a pizza joint, dry cleaner's, nail salon.

All closed.

He parks the van in the diagonal slot between lines and lets himself look at his watch.

Two minutes to spare.

Then he waits, knowing that they're watching
him.

110

Chon comes out of the water.
Creature from the Black Lagoon.
He hits land and walks back to where he parked
the pony.
Looks at his watch.
Four minutes.
He races down to Spanish Landing, where a row
of phone booths stand like monuments to the past.
Fumbles quarters into the slot and dials the
number he was told to dial.
'It's done.'

111

Ben's phone rings.
'Yes!'
Pull back on to Fairview, they tell him.
Go two lights, take a left.
Two more blocks, take a right.
Go now, we'll call back.
Ben drives, a new mantra in his shaken brain—
Two lights left, two more right.
Just before the second right, the phone rings again.
'See the fish store?'
Ben looks around . . .
The fish store, the—

—then sees the sign with the cartoon fish, bubbles coming up from his mouth; the place sells tropical fish for home tanks—

'Yes, I see it.'

'Take the right, then right into the alley behind the store.'

He does it.

Pulls in to the alley.

'Put it in park and get out.'

'Should I shut off the engine?'

'No.'

He does what he's told and gets out of the car.

It happens real fast. A car rolls in, two guys jump out the back. One of them grabs Ben, shoves him against the shop's back door, and presses a pistol to his head. The other snatches the phone out of his hand.

'One word, one move, one sound. You die quick, the girl dies slow.'

Ben nods as best he can with the hand around his neck, his cheek pressed against the metal door.

'You take our car, we take yours. We see anyone following us, we see a cop, a chopper, anything, the girl is dead.'

Ben nods again.

'Wait a minute and then go home. We'll call.'

The hand lets him go.

He hears the van drive off.

Ben gets into the car, a CRV. The keys are in the ignition. A duffel bag is set on the passenger seat. He opens it up and sees

Cash.

A lot of cash.

They paid for the dope.

Ben heads back to Laguna.

112

Chon comes in an hour later. Looks at Ben and nods.

Ben nods back.

They sit and watch the computer screen.

113

The cell phone rings.

Lado answers it.

O hears him talk in Spanish. Living where she lives she should know some Spanish but other than a little slang and taco stand items she doesn't. But the ugly Mexican is nodding and saying something that looks like 'I understand, I understand, sí, I understand.'

Then he puts the phone down and picks up the chain saw.

114

Do not send to ask for whom the bell tolls.

The little *bong* on the computer announces e-mail. Ben opens it and clicks on the provided link. Streaming video. Podcast.

O, alive, cuffed to the same wooden chair.

Her head slumped as she sobs.

A big man, hooded sweatshirt and shades, stands behind her with the chain saw, one hand on the starter cord.

'We did what you said!' Ben yells.

'Shut up,' Chon says quietly.

'We did what you said, let her go!'

'Now that we have learned a lesson, we're ready to move ahead in our relationship. Our demands are nonnegotiable. You will continue to grow your product and sell it to us at a price that we will set for a period of three years, commencing immediately. You will also provide certain services for us as we might require them. At the end of that contractual period, your obligations will be considered discharged.'

'Three years,' Ben says before he thinks to stop himself.

'It's been done.'

115

No shit it's been done.

To Chon, for example.

When Chon was ten, his father's partners kidnapped and held him for almost four months until Dad came up with the jack he owed them on a major marijuana shipment.

It wasn't so bad. They took him to some ranch they had way the hell out near Hemet and he watched television and played video games all day and most of the night. Let him shovel down Cap'n Crunch and Coca-Cola. They even let him drive around on this ATV they had until he went Steve McQueen on it and nearly plowed down a barbed-wire fence in an escape attempt.

They took *Penthouse* away from him for a week. Seriously bummed him out.

Anyway, Big John coughed the cash and got Little Johnny back. With the words 'See how much I love you? Four hundred K.'

Always nice to know your worth.

116

Ben, because he's Ben, comes up with another option.

(Ben is a big believer in Win-Win negotiations.)

He says, 'Figure out the profit you would realize over those three years, come up with a number and we'll pay it for her immediate release.'

117

'It's an interesting offer,' Elena says.
'He's no dummy,' Jaime observes.
Elena says—
'We'll get back to you.'

118

Because at the end of the day that's what it's all about.

The numbers.

They pencil or they don't.

Jaime gets on it. Very simple projection to make, based on present sales, market predictions, adjust for inflation, mix in a float for currency variations . . .

Anyone want to play *The Price Is Right?*

Come on down!

The price of three years of indentured servitude plus the life of one slightly messed up Laguna girl . . . without going over . . . is . . .

119

Twenty million dollars.

120

'It's a deal.'

'I want to be sure we understand each other – you will work for us, and the girl will be our guest for three years or until you remit a flat payment of twenty million dollars. Correct?'

'Yes.'

'Deal?'

'Deal,' Ben says.

'And how about Mr Fuck You?'

Chon nods.

'I want to hear you say it.' It's on the tip of his tongue

It is, it is.

He tries to control it, tries to stop it but

Chon says . . .

121

We have a deal.

122

A new vid-clip runs through O's head.

A continuous loop – she can't stop it, can't shut the auto-replay off. Can't change the settings.

It replays and replays and replays.

In the vid-clip she sees herself

Tied to a chair—

A chain saw at her neck

She feels the terror, the pure fear

She sees

The blade come toward her

She knows

Her own death

She hears

Herself scream.

Replay.

Blindfolded, it's worse because she can *only* see into her own head. Can't move around the multi-plex until she finds a movie she likes, she's just stuck with this one. She's always been 'the crazy girl,' but now she's seriously afraid she's going to become the *crazy* girl.

One thought keeps her half sane.

Her men are coming for her. She knows they are.

123

His baditude tamed

Chon nevertheless has a gun in his hand as he stands on the deck, looks out at the ocean, and doesn't really see it.

What he sees instead is

—himself killing people.

He would like to kill—

Hernan Lauter, and

The fucker who was holding the chain saw, and—

Hernan Lauter again.

Chon would like to start every day by killing Hernan Lauter and in a sense he does because he wakes up from what little sleep he gets by thinking about it. It's a little tricky to imagine it in detail, as he's never seen Lauter, but Chon goes with his mental image.

Sometimes Lauter is fat; others, skinny; young, old, jowly, sunken, various shades of brown or white skin, his hair is jet black, it's white, it's silver, it's thick or thin.

The method of killing him never varies, though.

Of course, of course in his fantasy Chon puts a pistol into Lauter's mouth and pulls the trigger.

Two shots—

—*bam bam*—

—then he gut-shoots the chain saw fucker, and while he is conveniently bent over Chon lops off his melon and tosses it at O's feet—

—gallant that he is—

Ever honest, Chon isn't really sure if his rage emanates more from what Hernan did to him or from what he did to O. Knows it should be the latter but is probably more the former because at the end of the day you really can't feel someone else's pain, you can only imagine it.

But he has a sense of what she feels because Lauter showed them both their imminent deaths.

His impotent – he selects the word deliberately – rage.

Because he knows that he can't actualize (there's a fucked-up non-word)

He can't act on

act *out*

his rage.

No amount of Viagra or Cialis will allow him to *actually* kill or even get within killing distance of Hernan Lauter. He's powerless to do it, so

his rage is an internal storm

brewing violently, getting stronger because it *is* contained

(tempest, teapot)

which, of course,

creates more
rage.

124

Ben walks out onto the deck.
Says, 'Maybe you were right.'
'Back when they first sent the threat,' Chon says.
'We should have either bugged out right then or
killed a bunch of people. That was a clean choice
and we didn't make it.'
'Too late now,' Ben says.
He breaks it down. They have Three Options:

1. Play Along – cooperate with the BC and
   hope O can stick it out for three years.
2. Find and Rescue – locate where they
   have O and go in and get her.
3. Pay the $20 mil.

The first option isn't an option. O could never
hack it that long, and besides, sooner or later Paqu
will want to know where her baby girl is and then
she'll go milk carton. The police, FBI, the whole
nine, and that will just get O killed.

The second option is unlikely. The BC could
have O anywhere, literally anywhere in the world.
If she's in Mexico, which is the most likely, there's
no way they're going to find her, much less go in
on some sort of Israeli-type raid and pull her out.
Not alive, anyway.

But they decide that they still have to try. One step at a time – try to locate her, but while they're doing that—

The next option – pay the freaking money.

Yeah, gladly, but they don't have that kind of cash, not liquid, anyway.

They have merchandise that they have to short-sell to the BC. Ben could sell the house, but who's buying multimillion-dollar houses these days? And banks are borrowing money, not lending it, and besides, what do you use as collateral – dope? In truth, better security than a lot of other things these days, but nothing you could put down on the loan application.

(You want to thaw the *frozen credit* freeze? Chon has asked. Make those cocksuckers who took our money and now won't lend it out again take their fists out of their pockets? Firing squads – you trot a few bank presidents out at half-time during *Monday Night Football,* machine-gun them on the fifty-yard line, and credit will flow like whiskey at an Irish wake.)

Ben has money – he has accounts in Switzerland, the Caymans, the Cooks. He has some investments that he can liquidate. The problem is, he has a lot of investments that he can't. Green Is Green. The guy is basically a one-man international aid organization, and he's put a lot of money where his mouth is. Darfur, Congo, Myanmar. So—

—liquidating everything he can liquidate, he can come up with

166

$15 million.

A shortfall of $5 million.

To free O.

'Do we know anyone with that kind of money?'
Ben asks.

'The Baja Cartel has that kind of money.'

The Baja Cartel *does* have that kind of money.

125

Where to begin, where to begin?

Ben, still Ben-like in his analysis, says they
should start with a review of their mistakes.

'Maoist self-criticism,' Chon offers.

'Something like that,' Ben says, and confesses to
the sins of—

Complacency.

Arrogance.

Ignorance.

Two will get you three.

But their complacency is at an end, likewise the
arrogance. Ignorance they're left with.

'Lauter knows everything about us,' Ben says.
'We know very little about him.'

So, first step.

126

The train comes.

Metrolink commuter, headed south for
Oceanside. Dennis walks over to the car.

'Twice inside a week,' he says. 'To what do I owe the pleasure?'

'Get in,' Ben says – invitation and demand.

Dennis slides into the passenger seat.

'I want all the information you have on the BC,' Ben says.

'I gave it to you.'

'I don't mean your freshman term paper,' Ben says. 'I mean your intel, your G-2, everything you have on the cartel.'

Dennis smirks. 'I can't do that.'

Ben smacks him across the face – hard.

'Jesus Christ, Ben! What the—'

This is Ben? Chon marvels.

Gentle Ben?

Increase-the-Peace Ben?

Cool.

'Actually, Dennis, you *can* do that,' Ben says. 'Or I *am* going to come to your office, knock on your boss's door, and introduce myself as the person who pays you more than he does.'

Dennis laughs. Ben and Dennis have this Mutually Assured Destruction thing going. They rat each other out, they end up in the same prison, and he reminds Ben of this perfectly symmetrical dynamic.

'I don't give a fuck anymore,' Ben growls, 'I'll go to jail. But you – your condo in Princeville gets auctioned off, your wife goes on welfare, and your kids go to the Assistant Manager Training Program at BK instead of to Bard.'

Dennis ain't laughing now. He's making excuses, though. 'You're talking thousands of pages—'

'Good.'

'Confidential informants—'

'All of it.'

'This isn't part of our deal,' Dennis says.

'It is now,' Chon says.

Dennis gets all blah-blah. What do you think I can do, just walk out of the building with crates of documents? It doesn't work that way. They watch you like *hawks,* it's *1984* in there with CCTV, internal spyware, all the updated technology.

'Dump it electronically,' Ben says. 'My computer geeks will call you. Follow their instructions. It won't take long.'

'It would take weeks for me to put this stuff together,' Dennis says.

'Listen, you double-dipping motherfucker,' Ben says. Then he goes Hyman Roth on him. 'We pay you every month, no excuses. We have a good month, we pay. A bad month, we pay. You don't ask and we don't say, because it's irrelevant. Year in, year out – we put your kids through school, we put clothes on their backs, food in their mouths. Now we need your fucking help and you're going to step up. Be at your computer at ten o'clock tonight, or at ten-oh-five . . .'

He recites Dennis's boss's cell phone number.

Dennis looks down at the car floor.

Sulking.

'I thought you were honorable people.'

'We're not,' Chon says.

'Start talking now,' Ben says. 'Give me something I can use on Hernan Lauter.'

Dennis laughs.

Hernan Lauter?

127

Hernan couldn't run a weed whacker, Dennis says. Hernan could *design* one, because he's a fucking engineer, but run the Baja Cartel, especially when they're at war? Please.

'So if Hernan isn't . . .'

'Elena La Reina,' Dennis happily answers.

Ben shrugs.

'Mommy.' Dennis is happy to surprise these two arrogant, condescending beach bums. 'His mother runs the show. Elena Sanchez Lauter, sister to the late unlamented Lauter brothers. Elena La Reina.'

128

'A female cartel boss?' Chon asks. 'In macho Mexico? I don't buy it.'

'Yeah,' Dennis says. 'I think it's *macho* Chon who rings up no purchase. I think you can't imagine what you can't imagine.'

May be the truth, Chon thinks.

Changes up the revenge fantasy, though.

Now he can't see himself doing it.

Although he's probably killed women before. Gone out on a scout, fingered an Afghan house with terrorists in it for the drone boys, there were probably women in it when it got vaporized.

But Chon won't hit a woman.

Can't see himself blowing one's brains out the back of her head, either.

Chauvinist pig.

Ben is amazed.

The head of the Baja Cartel is a woman?

Hillary would be pissed.

129

O isn't so thrilled, either.

That it was the *Pink* Power Ranger who was going to cut her freaking head off. She heard the woman's voice over the phone, giving orders to Chain Saw Guy.

So much for sisterhood.

Oprah ain't going to like this.

And if those verbally violent femmes on *The View* get hold of this bitch, look out.

130

Dennis gets out of the car, then looks back at them.

'If you're going up against Elena La Reina,' he says, 'I see dead people.'

It makes him feel a little better.

So does the double bacon burger

With cheese.

131

He has a point, so Chon and Ben hit the shooting range.

Chon goes to the range all the time not because he's preparing for the revolution or the Reconquista, not because he has phallic wet dreams about protecting home and hearth from burglars or home invasion. You gotta love 'home invasions' – we thought it would be Mexicans, turns out it was mortgage companies.

Chon likes shooting guns.

He likes the feel of metal in his hands, the kick, the blowback, the precision of chemistry, physics, and engineering mixed with hand-eye coordination. Not to mention power – shooting a gun projects your personal will across time and space in a flash. I want to hit that and that is hit. Straight from your mind to the physical world. Talk about your PowerPoint presentations.

You can spend fifty thousand years practicing meditation or you can buy a gun.

On the shooting range you create a neat, tiny hole in a piece of paper – the crisp entry but not the sloppy exit wound – and it's deeply satisfying. Anyway, Chon likes firearms, they are the tools

of his trade.

(The distinction, anthropologically speaking, between a 'tool' and a 'weapon' is that the former is used on inanimate objects and the latter on animate objects, if you can get with the concept of animate 'objects.')

Not so much Ben, who has been taught to loathe guns

And gun owners.

Who were, in his liberal home, the object of derision. Atavistic redneck goobers and right-wing crazies. His parents would shake their heads and chuckle sadly at the old bumper sticker *You'll take my gun when you pry it out of my cold dead hands.* How sad, how sad, how backward. *Guns don't kill people, people kill people.* (Guns do kill people, Chon says – that's what they're fucking for.) Yes, people with guns, Ben's father would opine.

Anyway, Ben is non-violent by nature.

132

'Impossible,' Chon argued with him one time. 'We're violent by nature, non-violent by training.'

'Other way around,' Ben countered. 'We're socially conditioned to be violent.'

'Look at chimps.'

'What about them?'

173

'We share ninety-seven percent of our DNA with chimps,' Chon said, 'and they're violent little fuckers who kill each other You can't tell me they're socially conditioned to do that.'

'Are you saying we're chimps?'

'Are you saying we're *not*?'

Of course we're chimps.

We're chimpanzees with guns.

Chon recalls some old saw about if you leave enough chimps in a room with enough typewriters eventually they'll bang out *Romeo and Juliet* and wonders if the same theory holds true for guns. If you left enough chimps in a room with enough MAC-10s, would they eventually all shoot each other?

All you'd really need is that one forward-looking chimp. That one sociopathic Cheetah with enough curiosity, brains, and inner rage to point the gun and pull the trigger and then it's on, man. Monkey see, monkey do – lead and pieces of Bonzo would be bouncing off those walls until the last chimp left standing (as it were) was mortally wounded.

Chon wonders if God (assuming a fact not in evidence) ever wondered, Hmmmm, if you leave enough humans on a planet with the atom, would they . . . Of course we fucking would, Chon knows, of course we fucking *will*, we fly airplanes into buildings intentionally, in the name of God. (Well, not in the name of 'God,' exactly, but . . .)

Anyway anyway, be that as it may.

Chon takes Ben to the firing range.

Which is filled today as usual with police types, military types, and women, a few of whom are police or military types.

OC women love shooting those guns, man. Maybe Freud was right, whatever, but they're in there with their earrings (off for the headsets) and jewelry and makeup and perfume blasting away at potential burglars, home invaders, rapists, and actual (okay, not actual) husbands, ex-husbands, boyfriends, lovers, fathers, step-fathers, male bosses, male employees who give them shit . . .

It's a truth-worn joke that women at firing ranges aim not for the head but the groin, that they're shooting not for the bull's eye but for the snake's eye until the instructors just give up and teach them to aim at the knees because that pistol is going to throw high so they'll catch boyfriend/hubby/daddy/ex-boyfriend/ex-hubby square in the junk.

Take O, for instance.

Chon took her to the range one day for giggles and shits.

The girl could shoot.

A natural.

(We mentioned that O likes power tools, right?)

She squeezed off six shots – two at a time, like Chon told her – and smacked each of them into fatal spots on the target. Lowered the pistol and said, 'I think I came a little.'

Now Chon hands Ben a pistol.

'Just point and shoot,' Chon tells him. 'Don't overthink it.'

Because Ben overanalyzes everything. Chon is surprised the boy can piss without succumbing to mental paralysis. (Would it be better to take my dick out with my right hand or my left hand? Would the choice of left hand have a subconscious connection to concepts of 'sinister,' as opposed to my right hand feeling 'dexterous,' and why is urine running down my leg?)

And truly, Ben is looking at the target silhouette and wondering if there are African-American shooting ranges where the target is a white figure on a field of black, a menacing KKKer coming out of the Mississippi night. Probably not. Not in the OC (which zealously guards its Second Amendment rights), anyway, where they should just put a sombrero on the targets and get it over with.

Take that, Pancho. And that, and that.

Ben hates this, how totally out of place he feels in this very weird, neo-fascist sandbox, looking at the black, albeit deracialized, silhouette figure staring menacingly at him as Chon is saying something about—

'Point and shoot twice.'

'Twice.'

Chon nods. 'Your hand-eye coordination automatically corrects for the second shot.'

176

'What should I aim at?' he asks Chon.

'Just hit the damn thing,' Chon answers. At the range they're probably thinking about, it won't matter, and anyway, hydrostatic shock is going to do the job. The bullet hits, creating a wall of blood that hits the heart like a tsunami wave – side out.

Ben points and shoots.

Twice.

Bam bam.

Misses the whole silhouette.

Twice.

So much for self-correction.

'You're going to have to get better at this,' Chon says. Recalling what his SEAL instructors said:

The more sweat on the training ground . . .

. . . the less blood on the battleground.

134

Well, O thinks

I got my own reality show, anyway

She looks up at the mounted video camera, high on the wall, that monitors her twenty-four seven.

The episode descriptions on the MTV website:

O gets DPed

O gets kidnapped

O is threatened with decapitation (or maybe O meets Jason)

O in captivity

Hostage O

Pretty much the first season.
Then set up the season-ending cliffhanger—
Will O survive or will O
Be eliminated?

135

Esteban is intrigued by the girl.
Of course he is, are you kidding?
Anglo chick, *guera, guapa,* and those tattoos running down her arm? A mermaid and shit? And those blue eyes?
She's a *bruja,* a witch, an enchantress.
No, don't get it wrong, Esteban isn't in love with her. Would his dick like to get up that? Sure – dicks have minds of their own. But he's in love with Lourdes, faithful to her and her swollen belly.
But he can't see her.
He can call her, but now Lado has him down here, taking care of the *guera* hostage. Bringing her meals, guarding her, making sure she don't get away. Lado, he was going to *cut this girl's head off*; Esteban is sure glad *that* didn't happen.
Doesn't know how he'd deal with that, he's still trying to get that other thing out of his head, the thing with that lawyer, squirming on the floor, begging, crying. Esteban can still see his own hand pulling the trigger, that lawyer's brains and hair blowing out the backside – he still wants to cry every time he thinks about that, which is a lot.

So he sure hopes Lado don't want him to do something to this girl.

She seems nice.

Loca, but nice.

136

Elena is somewhat intrigued by O herself.

Sometimes she sits at the computer and tunes in to the camera and watches her.

The girl has such a distinct, if odd, sense of style. Very personal, much too brave, the tattoo is bizarre but you have to admire the courage, the independence.

Elena truly hopes that she won't have to kill her.

137

Option one is Play and Obey, so—

Ben's first meeting with his new employers takes place in a room at the Surf & Sand, pricey but still cheaper than the Montage.

Alex and Jaime arrive accompanied by napalm.

That is, the smell of victory.

Smug, cloying, sickly, and obnoxious.

They come with something else: a middle-age Mexican they don't introduce by name but instead as the Man, the BC's CEO in the OC.

Ben is sorry Chon isn't there because he would fucking love that.

The BCCEOOC doesn't say anything, just looks

at Ben as A&J explain that everything they are about to tell him comes directly from the BCCEOOC, who has a pair of the coldest eyes that Ben has ever seen outside a hostage video.

Specifically the one starring O.

And this guy, whom Ben recognizes as Mr Chain Saw.

It is explained to Ben that:

He will give them the locations of his grow houses and

Inform them, through Alex, of when a crop is ready, at which time

The BC will send a crew to pick it up, with

The agreed-upon payment and in the meantime

Ben should start contacting his customers to acquaint them with the changes and make sure that they comply with the new order of things and

If Ben has any problems he should contact

Alex or Jaime, but it is sincerely hoped that Ben will *not* have any problems nor hopefully will the

BC have any problems with Ben, but if they do he will be contacted by Jaime or Alex and the problem will be quickly resolved or

He will see Mr. Chain Saw again, who *will* resolve the problem, by killing O.

Does Ben understand?

Ben does: Ben is to be the object of prison love, repeatedly, for three years or twenty million dollars. He gives them the location of a grow house with a harvest due date two days away.

This should give him time to plan.

180

A three-year sentence
O contemplates
Unless her boys come up with the Monet.
(O flunked Art History twice, partially because of her inability to distinguish Monet from Manet, partially because of her inability to get to class.) She does know money from Monet, though, enough to know that twenty mil is a lot of either, and while the boys wouldn't hesitate to fork it over if they have it, she doesn't think they have it.
Yet.
So she's going to do some time.
For a brief but interesting period in her young life, O had a thing for Women's Prison Movies. She and Ash used to sit up and watch old videos. *Chained Heat, Canned Heat, Chained Canned Heat.* Anyway, there was always some young chick who got thrown in with a bunch of hard-core dykes, a rapacious male or female warden, and a kinder, older mother-figure prisoner and O and Ash got off on the soft-core lesbian porn. Their favorite thing to do was turn the sound off and make up the dialogue themselves.
So she thinks she knows a little about doing time.
At least they took the blindfold off. Put her in a room with a bed, a chair, an attached bathroom with a toilet, sink, and shower. There's a window, but they taped over it so she can't look

outside and take a guess as to where the fuck she is.

And, of course, the one door is locked from the outside.

Three times a day this sweet, shy Mexican kid comes in with a meal on a tray. O has asked, but the kid won't tell her his name.

Breakfast is always a roll with butter and strawberry jam.

Lunch is a peanut butter and jelly sandwich.

Dinner is a microwave whatever.

This isn't going to work.

Not for three freaking years if it comes to that.

For one thing, the video replay is driving her nuts.

Two, when that isn't playing she's bored out of her skull.

So . . .

She starts taking her head out for little walks.

139

Later that night

Ben and Chon sit in the office on Brooks Street watching Jeff and Craig do-do the computer voodoo.

Jeff, clad in board trunks and a T-shirt, leans back in his chair with the lappie on his, uhhh, lap, and his bare feet up on the desk. He sucks on a joint and looks at the screen, while Craig, on the headset, talks Dennis through it.

Craig is dressed formally for the occasion – jeans, tennis shoes, a shirt with sleeves. He puts his hand over the mike, smiles, and says, 'Your boy is nervous.'

'Can you break through the DEA firewall?' Ben asks.

Craig rolls his eyes. Jeff smiles and says, 'We know the guys who wrote the software. Nice dudes, but . . .'

'Got him,' Craig says.

He spins his chair so Ben can see the screen.

'Easy squeezy now,' Craig says into the mike. 'I'm looking at what you're looking at.'

He starts speaking geek – combos of numbers and letters, 'alt' this, 'enter' that. Every once in a while he breaks into an Indian accent because he thinks it's funny. ('Just trying to dial down the vibe.') It isn't. About twenty minutes later Craig says into the phone, 'Okay, hit the button and you give me the joystick.'

Dennis does.

'It's Amazon now,' Jeff says to Ben. 'Happy shopping.'

140

O creates a new persona for herself.

Tragic heroine.

As opposed to tragically hip heroin girlfriend, a previous fantasy involving Chon's non-existent addiction.

It's nice to move to center stage, though, or center scaffold, as long as it doesn't actually happen, instead of being the supportive woman you've seen in a few thousand movies and TV shows.

So she models herself on Famous Women Who Have Been Beheaded, or more accurately, Women Who Are Famous for Being Beheaded because, like, none of these babies would have gotten a mention except for their spectacular exit scenes.

O consults history for this.

Which is a task because she's never really read any. All O's background study for this role comes from movies and TV, of which she's seen a lot a lot.

Anyway, she makes a (mental) list:

Marie Antoinette, of course.

Good clothes – the chick could shop. You turn MA loose in South Coast Plaza or Fashion Valley, you got something going.

O is familiar with Marie (they're on first-name status now, based on shared experience) mainly from the movie with Kirsten Dunst. The movie had very cool music – New Order, the Cure, Siouxsie and the Banshees – and Marie was married at age fourteen and couldn't get her husband to do her until she finally explained to him it was like a key going into a lock, which apparently got him enthused. But then she got into a lot of trouble for eating a bunch of pastries and throwing parties, which O can relate to because Paqu approved of neither of these things. The movie didn't actually show Marie getting her head cut off, but O remembers something about that from history class in high school and also something about the girl saying, 'Let 'em eat cake,' which, you know, you'd think would be a happy thing, but you never know what's going to piss off the French.

So there's Marie and there's Anne Boleyn, whom O knows from the TV series and from a movie about her sister. The girl was a real slut, apparently. She fucked a lot of guys, including maybe even her own brother. O doesn't hold the slut thing against her – she's fucked a lot of guys, too, and never had a brother (one pregnancy was plenty for Paqu, thank you. She went out and got her tubes tied after O), so who knows?

Anyway, the chick in the series was fucking *hot*. This catlike little body and she was, like, dirty girl, and O and Ash were very into her and *very* into the guy playing Henry VIII so when they hooked up it was OMFG. But then VIII got tired of her and she couldn't produce a boy and they sentenced her to death for fucking her brother and some other guy and she came out of the Tower looking all demure and shit and kneeled in front of the chopping block and stretched her arms out and she had this beautiful, elegant neck, but when it comes to beautiful necks you have to give the trophy to Natalie Portman, who played Anne in the movie and Anne was a *major* cocktease. Which O never really mastered but never really tried because she just really likes cocks so why pretend otherwise?

So there's Marie Antoinette and Anne Boleyn.

There was Catherine somebody, but that's season four and it hasn't been on yet so O doesn't know anything about her.

Then there was Lady Jane Grey, played in this old movie by that chick who was in the Harry Potter movies, and she was queen for just nine days, which is a bummer and O can't remember why they chopped her head off, just that they did.

Mary, Queen of Scots.

O is pretty sure she was decapitated because she read something about Scarlett Johansson was going to star in the movie, but something happened and they didn't make the movie, which O thinks was a mistake because a lot of mammarily challenged chicks, herself included, would have happily laid down ten bucks to see Scarlett get her head cut off.

O decides to go with Marie Antoinette.

Let 'em eat cake.

141

The problem with intelligence is not *what*, it's *which*. It's too *much* info, not not enough. You have to somehow find what's significant. So now that they have piles of shit on the Baja Cartel, stored on five thumb-drives – they have to sift through it to find what they need.

The speed helps.

Yeah, used to be a coffee-and-cigarette deal, the all-night research thing, the two intrepid investigative reporters looking for Deep Throat, the buddy cops going after that one clue before the lieutenant shuts them down because he's getting heat from the mayor's office.

Fuck that.

They don't smoke (cigarettes) and Ben already has the shits without making it worse by jacking a bunch of Italian Roast and anyway, he'd just buy that fair trade crap that tastes like dirt so they go the pharmacological route.

Chemical toothpicks for the eyes.

Pop. Pop.

Sitting in front of a computer on speed is like putting the car in park while you stomp the gas pedal through the floor.

Idling at a buck ten.

She can't take much more, Captain.

Yeah, well, she could, Jim, if she had Ben to hook her up with an *indica-sativa* blend that puts your nerves in park while leaving your brain in high gear.

Dawn finds them—

Check that—

Dawn doesn't 'find' shit – dawn's not looking. (The only redeeming quality of the universe, Chon believes, is its indifference.)

When the sun comes up they're still there, poring over the mass of material.

Ben, natch, wants context.

'There is no *content* without con*text*,' he says. Something he picked up at Berkeley.

Chon's hoping that Ben doesn't want to 'deconstruct' the Baja Cartel. Chon wants to deconstruct the cartel, but in a very different, non-Derrida way. Context, content – he didn't want to go down this road, but as long as they are, he just wants to go in and blast people.

He's a little cranky without any sleep. But Chon knows from experience that it's a Big Mistake, trying to sleep after a speed binge.

You can't rope that pony, you gotta let it run until it drops on its own. (Warning: trying to sleep on speed may trigger a psychotic episode. Consult your physician immediately. Like, warning: if erection persists for more than four hours, consult a physician immediately and hope you have one fucking horny physician.)

Ben's not deconstructing the cartel, he's deconstructing the information. It looks like Dennis has gotten most of his intel from a single source – CI 1459, who isn't identified anywhere in the file.

So Dennis isn't giving that shit up to anybody, not even his own people. Not uncommon – an asset is just that, an asset, and bureaucrats don't give their coins away.

We'll get it when we need it, Ben thinks.

'Okay, so what's your fucking context?' Chon asks.

142

The Lauter family consisted of four brothers and three sisters.

Chekhov, take note.

Elena was smack in the middle.

He finds a photo of Elena.

Definite MILF.

Ebony hair, high cheekbones, deep brown eyes, tight little body.

Queen Elena.

One by one, she watched her brothers go down. The only male left in the family is her boy, Hernan, but it's not him, he's not that guy, he's not capable. He's an engineer, he's smart, he could learn the business aspect, but he's not really serious about the engineering or anything else, except maybe pussy.

Mommy knew this, she knew that he couldn't run the family business, part of her would have liked to just get out and let EL Azul and Sinaloa have the fucking thing. But she also knew that as the last dick left standing his rivals couldn't let her son live.

She had to take over, if only to keep him alive.

She didn't want to find him in a barrel of acid.

She's the most capable. She has the brains, the experience, the name, the DNA, the spine, the guys, the sangfroid, the balls and/or the ovaries.

And she finds that she likes running things, likes the power.

Elena's hot – sexy, good-looking, smart, efficient. She uses all that to keep loyal supporters around her. She's also ruthless – it's love me or off with your head. She's the Red Queen.

Azul, a former lieutenant, can't take it. Just won't let himself be bossed around by a woman, plus he doesn't think she can do it. Probably doesn't think she can drive or balance a checkbook, either, so he breaks off and forms his own thing. Goes back to the rednecks in Sinaloa and says, 'Can you believe that, the Lauters are led by a woman, what's going to happen when she goes on the rag, huh?'

'I'll tell you what freaking happens,' Ben says, warming to the subject, 'guys get their freaking heads cut off, blood's going to flow, all right.'

But Elena is smart – she grew up in the drug trade, there's nothing she hasn't seen before, so she does a cold-blooded analysis and sees she's going to lose in a war with El Azul and Sinaloa.

A recent analysis, written by Dennis, suggests that the Elena/Hernan section of the BC is allied with a group called Los Zetas.

'The vid-clip boys,' Chon says.

Los Zetas recently have branched out across the border into California and formed a subgroup called Los Treintes. DEA doesn't seem to know much about them, but they appear to be headed up by a former Zeta named Miguel Arroyo Salazar, aka 'El Helado' – 'Stone Cold.'

Ben shows Chon the old photo in the file showing a Baja State Police officer. They pull up the recording of the hostage video and look at the man with the chain saw standing next to O.

'Same guy?' Ben asks.

'Looks like it.'

'Same guy I met with today,' Ben says. 'Our new boss – Miguel Arroyo Salazar.'

'He's a dead fucker,' Chon says. Sooner or later, he's going.

So, Ben continues, Elena recruits Zeta – pays them well, gives them their own turf to use, and tells them, 'Go forth and prosper.' Go north, young men, and take California (back).

'Why?' Ben asks rhetorically.

'Because that's where the money is,' Chon answers rhetorically.

Or is it something else? Ben ponders.

He lets that slide, though.

First things first and the first thing is to get O back alive.

Buy her back.

'We have enough here to move on,' Chon says.

191

Fuck context.

Let's get to con*tent*.

143

We have to be careful, Ben thinks.

We have to be beyond careful. If the BC gets one whiff that we're using their own money to pay them, they'll kill O.

So—

144

They find the address in one of Dennis's files.

Way out in the new eastern housing developments that hug the mountains.

Cougar country.

Not the *new* kind of cougar, the *old* kind of cougar, actual big cats.

Dennis has had it under watch for months. Rented by one Ron Cabral, a known associate, etc.

Now Ben and Chon have it up.

They watch the cars come and go, late at night or early in the morning, usually before dawn. They get a sense of when the runs are made, when deliveries come in, go out, how many men.

Stash house.

Where money is kept until it's packed up and delivered south.

Or not, as the case may be.

Chon parks the Mustang two miles away and hikes in through the thick chaparral on the hillsides.

Feels almost good to be humping it again.

He plops his ass down, gets out the nocs, and scopes the terrain until he finds what he's looking for – a sharp curve in the road away from the houses. Takes a mental snapshot and stores it.

I-Rock-and-Roll, Stanland, SoCal.

An ambush is an ambush.

Is an ambush.

146

They go over it a gazillion times.

In Ben's opinion.

Not enough in Chon's.

'It's no fucking game,' Chon says.

'Didn't say it is,' Ben responds. 'What I'm saying is I got it. It's in my head.'

Yeah, but Chon knows it goes out of your head the second the action starts and the adrenaline kicks in. Then it's all muscle memory that comes from repetition, repetition, repetition.

So they go over it again.

147

O makes the rounds of the talk shows.

O-prah, of course.

OPRAH
. . . a story of courage, of . . . inspiring . . .
dignity. Please welcome O.

The audience applauds. A few stand. 0, demure in a
gray dress, walks out, shyly acknowledges the applause,
and sits down.

OPRAH
What a truly amazing experience. What did you
learn? What did you take away?

O
Well, Oprah, you know, when you're alone that
long you have no choice but to confront yourself. I think you gain a self-knowledge. You really
learn about yourself.

OPRAH looks to the women in the audience and
smiles. 'Isn't this girl amazing?' She turns back to O.

OPRAH
(softly)
What did you learn?

O
How strong I really am. How strong a woman . . .
an inner strength that I hadn't fully realized . . .

194

Applause.

OPRAH

Next, a truly awe-inspiring example of courage
under pressure – O's mother, Paqu.

O moves on to Ellen.

ELLEN

Give it up for MTV's O!

O, in a jaunty sleeveless T-shirt that displays her tattoos,
breaks out a few dance moves and then plops down in
the guest chair.

ELLEN

You've had quite a time of it, haven't you?

O

Oh yeah. But first – you get to do Portia de
Rossi? I'd trade jerseys for that.

The audience cracks up.
She dances with ELLEN, then

On to Dr Phil.

DR PHIL

. . . the best predictor of future behavior is past
behavior, and I'm a big believer that you teach
people how to treat you. You have to consent

to be a hostage, and if you don't own your part in this then you have no power to fix it. I've been doing kidnap and hostage cases for thirty-five years, I didn't just fall off the turnip truck. For every rat you see there are fifty you don't.

O

You're a fucking asshole.

DR PHIL

I'm prepared to offer you first-class help if you'll take it. But I'm not playing games here, we're going to drill down and get to the bottom of this, I'm just an old country boy—

O

And an asshole.

Oh, girl, she tells herself – you have to get it together.

148

Ben drops Chon off at Seizure World—

—a retirement community really called Leisure World, so you figure it out—

—after midnight when the old people are asleep, but before 4:00 AM, when they all wake up again—

—and Chon walks around until he finds a Lincoln he likes. It takes him eighteen seconds to

196

jimmy the door, another thirty to hot-wire it ('fruits of a misspent youth'), and he drives it away and hides it in a strip mall parking lot in SJC, where Ben picks him up.

'You know what you get when you cross a Mexican with a Chinese?' Chon asks.

'What?'

'A car thief who can't drive.'

149

'You okay?' Chon asks.

'I'm stoked,' Ben answers.

'Don't be *too* stoked,' Chon says. 'Smoke up, chill.'

'That would be okay?'

'Yeah.'

Chon doesn't fucking know if it would be okay. He's gone on night missions before but not like this one. Guesses it's pretty much the same, though. You want to be wired, but not too wired.

Ben just looks nervous, edgy.

But determined in that serious Ben way.

They smoke up, a selected *indica-sativa* blend that will smooth them out but still leave them alert.

Just to take the edge off.

They drive to the stolen Lincoln and head out.

East on Highway 74, aka the Ortega Highway, traversing (Chon likes that word) the Santa Ana Mountains from Mission Viejo to Lake Snore—

Etymology:

Lake Elsinore—

it's a sleepy little town, ya—

Lake Snore.

The Ortega is about as rural as you get in Orange Country anymore and it's a good place for grow houses (relevant) and meth labs (irrelevant, at the moment, anyway). They turn north onto one of the many narrow roads that run off the spine of the highway like broken ribs through forests of post oaks.

They pull the car over onto a dirt . . . pullover . . . at a stop sign by a T-junction.

Chon gets out and ties a red rag to the car's door handle, opens the hood, and rips out the battery cables. He gets back in and tells Ben to lie down on the seat and put the mask on.

Ben went to Party City in Costa Mesa and decided on a talk-show theme. So here they are – Leno, Letterman – waiting to do their opening monologue.

Now his hand flexes on the butt of the pistol in his lap.

'You only use that,' Chon says, 'if you have to.'

'No shit.'

'No different than a v-ball game,' Chon says. 'Focus and teamwork.'

Few minutes later they hear a car coming up the road.

'You ready?' Chon asks.

Ben's throat closes up.

Chon feels nothing.

The van slows for the stop sign. The guard in the passenger seat sees the broken-down Lincoln but doesn't think a thing about it until the car suddenly pulls in front of the van and blocks the road.

Chon is out of the car in a fucking flash.

Has the shotgun pointed at the driver's window.

The driver starts to put it in reverse, but Chon aims at his head and the driver changes his mind. The passenger goes for the pistol on the seat but Ben is at his window with the .22 trained on him.

'Drop it,' Ben says, which he's heard in about a thousand TV shows so it almost makes him giggle to say it. But the guy drops the gun on the floor of the car.

Chon opens the door, grabs the driver, and jerks him out and onto the ground as Ben gestures for the passenger to get out. The passenger does, looks at Ben, and says in Spanish, 'You don't know who you're fucking with. We're with La Treinte.'

Ben points the gun to the ground, like, get down.

The passenger yawns elaborately to show he's not scared, then eases himself onto the ground, trying to keep the red dirt off his white shirt.

Chon keeps the shotgun on the driver while Ben gets into the van and quickly finds the money. He also finds the GPS tracking device stuck in there with the cash and tosses it on the ground.

Says, '*Vamanos.*'

Chon shoots twice, into the front and back tires of the van.

Then they get into the Lincoln and take off.

150

'That was so *cool*!'

Ben is lit freaking up.

Adrenaline high. Endorphins bouncing off the cell walls like a schizophrenic playing racquetball against himself. Like nothing he's ever experienced.

'Count it,' Chon says.

$765,500.

A start.

151

'We found the Lincoln,' Hector tells Lado.

Lado shrugs. 'Where?'

'Parking lot at the San Juan train station,' Hector answers. 'It's registered to a Floyd Hendrickson. He's eighty-three years old and reported it stolen this morning.'

They go to talk to the driver and the *pendejo* who was riding shotgun.

Lado and Hector take them to a big date farm out near Indio and put them in a shed where they keep tractors and shit. The two sit on the dirt floor leaning against the corrugated-tin wall and they develop verbal diarrhea. Keep shitting on and on about how there were two of them, a shotgun and two pistols, real pros . . .

Lado already knows they were pros – they knew when, where, and what, and they knew to look for the GPS.

'Two of them? You sure?' Lado asks.

They're really sure.

Two tall guys.

Lado thinks that's interesting.

Wearing masks.

'What kind of masks?'

Yanqui television hosts.

Jay Leno and . . .

'Letterman,' the driver says.

The other one got the car make and license plate.

'It's a wonder,' Lado says, 'that neither of you two got hurt at all.'

Very fortunate, they agree.

Yeah, well, *that* ain't gonna last.

152

Lado is pretty sure they're telling the truth and had nothing to do with it.

Other than being stupid, lazy cowards and letting it happen.

These *cabróns* have families down in Mexico, SOP for anyone working for the BC on this side of the border – you have to have family where the BC can reach out and touch them.

Fuck job references – you want to guarantee good performance and loyalty you keep parents, brothers and sisters, even cousins in your pocket. Men who think nothing of risking their own lives would never think of risking their families'.

He tosses the bullwhip to the ground.

Two tall guys . . .

No, it's not likely. How would the two *gueros* know the location of the stash house, the route the drivers take?

They couldn't.

No, a *tombe* like this has to be an inside job. Maybe not these two *pendejos*, but someone inside.

'Cut them down,' he snaps.

153

Designer coffee joint on Ritz-Carlton Drive.

And the PCH, coast side.

Chon refers to the place as Yummy Mummy Heaven.

Useta park himself at one of the outdoor tables, sip cappuccinos, and watch the parade of rich young mommies jog past pushing their three-wheeled running strollers. Tight bodies in T-shirts (or designer hoodies, in colder weather) and sweatpants.

'That's the early shift,' he explained to Ben.

The later shift involves the exclusive day care just up the street. The slightly older YMs would drop the brats off and then come in for their lattes and, maybe, post-latte sex with Chon.

'Bored and resentful,' Chon observed to Ben. 'Perfect in bed.'

'Adulterer.'

'I'm not married.'

'What ever happened to morality?' Ben sighed.

'Same thing that happened to CDs.'

Replaced by a newer, faster, easier technology.

Ben asked, 'What would O think about these squalid escapades?'

'You kidding?' Chon answered. 'She talent-spots for me.'

'Shut up.'

No, it's truth. O, when she can get up that early, has spent many happy hours handicapping Chon's odds. That one's hot, that one's horny, that one is happy at home, forget her, check out that ass, I'd do *that* one . . .

'Did she ever . . .'

'Nah.'

They're not thinking about O's barely latent lesbian tendencies or Yummy Mummys this morning. They're thinking about O, however, as

Alex and Jaime walk in—

'Siamese beaners.'

'Easy.'

—stand at the counter and order coffee to go.

Ben and Chon follow them out to the parking lot and get in the backseat of Alex's Mercedes.

'What?' Ben asks.

Alex turns around to look at Ben. 'One of our cars was hijacked last night.'

Ben is stone. The son of two incessantly probing shrinks, he knows how to outface an interrogation.

'So?'

Alex is an amateur at this.

Shows all over his lawyer face. 'Would you know anything about it?'

Ben jumps all over the conditional tense. 'Yeah, I *would* know something about it, if I had anything to do with it. Seeing as how I didn't, I don't.'

Fun with language.

Alex tries Chon for a stare-down.

Yeah, that's going to work.

Try making a Rottweiler blink.

'Okay,' Alex says finally.

Chon is Chon but Ben is Ben. 'Try not calling me out for nonsense in the future, okay? How is O?'

'Who?'

'Who'? Chon looks like he might slap the guy. It's a real possibility there for a second, but Ben jumps in. 'Ophelia. We call her O. The young lady you kidnapped. How is she? We want to talk to her.'

'Maybe that can be worked out,' Alex says.

Ben notices the passive verb form.

Responsibility is being avoided, or

Authority is not possessed.

Interesting.

'Work it out,' Ben says. He opens the car door. 'If there's nothing else, Chon has marriages to destroy and I have product to produce.'

They stand in the parking lot as the Mercedes pulls away.

'You're good,' Chon says. 'You think they really suspect us?'

'If they did, we'd have seen Chain Saw Guy.'

204

They walk back to the shop.

'By the way?' Chon says. 'I feel I make the marriages better.'

'Really?'

'Oh yeah.'

154

The myth about drug-trade hijacking is that it's the perfect crime because the victims can't report the theft to the police.

Uhhhhhhhh . . .

They might not file a police *report,* but that doesn't mean they won't report it to the police.

It just has to be the right police.

Alex happens to know a few.

For example, Deputy Brian Berlinger of the Orange County Sheriff's Department has a nice A-frame in Big Bear that he likes to go to on weekends and holidays. Which is why right now he's on his computer researching which stores in the OC stock Leno and Letterman masks.

155

For the next hijacking, Ben decides on movie stars.

'I think I'm going gay,' he tells Chon.

'No surprise, but specifically . . .'

'I'm frighteningly into this *theme* thing,' Ben says as he looks at his choices on an Internet catalog.

'If the dope and robbery don't work out, maybe I could go into event planning.'

'Or suck cock.'

'There's always that,' Ben admits. He studies the offerings. 'You want to be Brad Pitt or George Clooney?'

'*Beyond* gay. You make gay look straight.'

'Choose.'

'Clooney.'

Ben hits 'Buy.'

Chon's on his own lappie.

Google Earth.

Aerial view of the next crime scene.

156

They'll be looking for it this time.

They'll be alert.

No shit.

Lado has put the word out, you see something on the side of the road, you don't stop, you don't slow down, you hit the gas, *ese*.

You keep driving, no matter what.

157

Ben and Chon finish laying the spike strip across the dirt road, and then shovel a light layer of gravel across it.

Like everybody else, they watch *Cops*. ('Bad boys, bad boys, whachoo gonna do . . .')

Then they go back to the work car, pulled off into an avocado field near Fallbrook.

'Guacamole?' Ben asks.

Yeah, okay, not funny.

The pregame nerves are starting to kick in. Chon's jaws look like they're tightened with an Allen wrench and Ben's knee bobs up and down like a jackhammer with a bad jones.

Yeah, but he gets off on it.

Why they call it 'high-jacking,' he thinks. He gets high jacking.

Ben hears car tires on the dirt road.

'Game,' Chon says.

They hear the tires pop, Chon pulls the work car onto the road, and they're *on* them. Same drill (practice, practice, practice) – Chon on the driver, Ben on the rider.

And it goes like that.

158

820K is a crap payday for Clooney and Pitt.

Lunch money for the *Ocean's* boys, but not bad for a jacking among the avocados.

159

'Brad Pitt and who?' Lado asks.

'George Clooney,' the driver says.

'*Ocean's Eleven*,' the rider adds.

'And *Twelve*.'

'Shut your stupid fucking mouth.'

He gets on the phone to Alex.

How are we coming on those masks?

160

They've narrowed it down to five stores and Berlinger is checking them out.

Is the answer to that question.

Lado drives to the parking lot at Aliso Beach.

'What?' Ben asks. Haven't I been—

    —producing my dope, haven't I been—

    —turning over my retailers, haven't I been—

    —talking to my customers, haven't I been—

    a good boy?

Lado looks Ben in the eyes. 'Where were you last night?'

Ben doesn't blink.

Lado's looking, too, *ese*. His black eyes have stared a lot of men down, seen the lies in their eyes, on the street, in the rooms, seen them lie hanging from meat hooks. Hard to look back into those black eyes and lie.

But Ben does. 'I was home. Why?'

'One of our cars was hit last night.'

Ben toughs it out. Keeps his eyes right on Lado's. 'We had nothing to do with it.'

'No?'

'No,' Ben says. 'Maybe you should look at your own people.'

Lado snorts.
Meaning—
My people know better.

161

Fuck yes they do.
Three years ago, two of his people staged an inside job on a cocaine processing lab in National City.
Carlos and Felipe thought they were real cute, thought they got away with it.
Turns out no.
Lado took them to a warehouse in Chula Vista. Made Carlos watch as he put Felipe into a burlap bag, tied the bag closed, and hoisted him up by a rafter.
Then played piñata.
Beat that bag with a stick until blood and bits of bone spilled on the floor like coins and candy.
Carlos confessed.

162

Ben looks bored.
Indifferent.
Forcing into his head the thought—
      You want to frighten me with horror
      stories? Come to the Congo, asshole.
Come to Darfur.
                  See what my eyes have
                  seen and then

209

Scare me with stories.

Lado doesn't try to scare him with stories. He says, 'If I track this back to you, your *putana* is dead.'

Ben knows that the slightest look of fear in his eyes, Lado will know.

So he looks him in the eyes and thinks

Fuck you.

163

Chon follows Lado away from the meeting.

Man drives to an apartment complex down in Dana Point Harbor, goes in, and is there for about an hour.

Chon thinks about going in after him. Do it right here, right now.

But knows he can't.

Lado comes out the same time as a woman. Nice-looking babe, maybe thirty, maybe not yet. Lado gets into his car, the gash gets into hers.

Chon makes a mental note of her license plate, then picks Lado up.

Tracks him to a landscaping company in SJC.

Lado goes into the office in back.

So when he's not trimming heads, Chon thinks, He trims hedges.

164

'We'd better do something,' Ben says. To deflect the suspicion a little.

'Such as?'

'Well,' Ben says. 'They're robbing us, right?'

'You could say so.' They've taken from us every-thing they could steal. (Apologies to Mr Dylan.)

'Then *we* need to rob us to show them they can't get away with it.'

(Apologies to Mr Sahl.)

165

Gary is the grower at this house out in the eastern part of Mission Viejo near the hills, a nice bespectacled twentysomething bio-geek who discovered you could make a lot more money with a lot less hassle creating designer dope for Ben than teaching Botany 101 to a bunch of freshmen who don't want to learn about it in the first place.

'Is it ready to go?' Chon asks Gary.

'It is,' Gary affirms, frowning. Gary is not happy about selling his fine, sophisticated labor of love over to the BC, whom he considers uncouth corporate barbarians incapable of appreciating the nuanced tones of this particular blend.

'Take the night off,' Chon says. 'We'll handle it.'

'Really?' Gary asks, grateful.

'Go on, you knucklehead,' Ben says. 'Get out of here.'

Gary gets out of there.

An hour later, the BC pickup boys arrive.

Quick transaction.

Cash for dope.

They wait a few minutes after they leave, then Ben says

'Stick 'em up.'

Then, 'Oh yeah . . . this is a robbery.'

'Cut the shit.'

But Ben is on a roll. 'Down on the floor. No mistakes, no one gets hurt. Don't anyone try to be a hero, and everyone goes home to their wife and kids.'

Chon says, 'Enough.'

Ben gets on the phone to Alex and says he has a problem.

166

'You rip me off *and* you rip me off?' Ben complains. 'Christ, Alex, there's greed and then there's greed, but to beat me on the price and then come in and jack the short money you *did* pay me, that's a hundred percent discount, which is a little much.'

They sit across from each other at a picnic table outside Papa's Tacos in South Laguna. If you want a really good fish taco you go to Papa's. If you don't, you go somewhere else.

'What are you talking about?' Alex asks.

'Five freaking minutes after your guys picked up the stuff,' Ben hisses, 'another set of guys came in and took the money.'

'You can't be serious.'

'Do I look like I'm kidding?'

Alex goes lawyer. 'Hey, after the transfer is made, it's not our responsibility.'

'Except that it was an inside job.'

Which is technically true.

'What makes you think it was an inside job?' Alex asks, getting a little pale.

'Who else knew?'

'Your people.'

Ben says, 'I've been in business for eight years and never been ripped off by *my* people.'

'What did the guys look like?'

'Well, they weren't retarded,' Ben says, 'because they were wearing masks.'

'What kind of masks?'

'Madonna and Lady Gaga.'

'This is not a time for jokes.'

'I agree,' Ben says. 'They didn't say a lot, but the little they did say sounded a little south of the border to me.'

Alex thinks about this for a second, but doesn't want to yield position. He says, 'Maybe you need to beef up your security.'

'And maybe,' Ben says, wrapping his taco and getting up, 'you need to look into yours. Get back to me on this. It better not happen again.'

Alex decides to go on the offensive. 'Do you have the ransom money yet?'

'Still working on it,' Ben snaps.

'He's all over me,' Alex says to Lado.

Pantry of one of Machado's taco stands in SJC. Alex doesn't like it – it smells like raw chicken and raw chicken is full of dangerous bacteria. He tries not to let his jacket touch the counter.

Lado sees his discomfort and enjoys it.

The Muppie *pendejo* should remember where he came from.

'So what?' Lado asks.

'He blames us.'

'So?'

'He's all over me.'

'You said that already.'

A kid comes in looking for a can of crushed tomatoes. Lado looks at him like he's nuts and the scared kid backs out.

'You sent the guys,' Alex says. 'Is it possible one or two of them are in business for themselves?'

'I'll look into it.'

'Because it's causing a prob—'

'I said I'd look into it.'

Lado's in an ugly mood, was when he woke up in the morning, is now, probably will be when he goes to bed. Delores started in on him when he was barely awake – the *fugeda* gutters need cleaning, Junior got a D in algebra, running her mouth just to hear herself talk.

He wants to scream at her – I have real problems. Another *tombe* . . .

Then three *cabróns* didn't show up for work this morning and he had to run down to the strip mall and hire three wetbacks from the parking lot. And now this pain in the balls? The *gueros* bitching because they're getting held up? Welcome to the club.

'I'll look into it,' he repeats. He walks out of the pantry, gets a burrito and some juice to go, and gets back in the car. It's already twelve-thirty and Gloria only gets an hour for lunch. She's a hairstylist in a shop down in Dana Point Harbor, but luckily her place is practically across the street.

He has a key and she's in bed waiting for him when he gets there. Wearing just the dark brown bra and panties he likes her in, the set he bought her that shows off her firm tits and that bubble ass.

'You're late, baby,' she says.

'Over.'

She turns over onto her elbows and knees.

Lado undresses, then kneels on the bed behind her and jerks the panties down around her ankles. He's proud that he's hard without her touching him or his touching himself – it's good for a man his age.

He runs his fingers over her back and feels her shiver. Her skin is like butter. Then he opens her up. Pounds her until she whimpers with pleasure and he feels the buildup in his balls and then he pulls out and flips her over.

She takes him in her mouth and finishes him with her hand.

Lado won't wear a condom and he don't want no more babies.

When Gloria comes out of the bathroom she lies down beside, runs her hand across his hair, and says, 'You're getting shaggy. You should come in for a cut.'

'I will.'

She gets up and starts to get dressed. 'I have a two o'clock.'

'Forget it.'

'"Forget it," he says. I have to work.'

'I'll pay it.'

'She's a regular.'

The black blouse fits tight over her tits. He bets she gets a lot of tips from the male customers. It should make him jealous, but it gets him hot instead, and she knows that. Sometimes she tells him she sees them get hard, brushes a thigh against theirs.

'I'll bet their wives really get it that night,' he says.

She says, 'I'll bet they do.'

Now she kisses him goodbye and leaves. He puts his pants on, goes into the kitchen, and pulls a beer from the refrigerator. Sits down and watches some stupid talk show on television.

It's nice to relax for a few minutes.

Then his cell phone rings and it's Delores.

Gloria comes into the shop and puts on the black smock. Teri, grabbing a cup of coffee, smirks at her.

'Why do I do it,' Gloria asks, 'when it just makes me feel dirty and degraded?'

'You just answered your own question,' Teri says.

Lado sits in the bleachers behind home plate and watches Francisco's setup. His feet are too close together, and Lado makes a mental note to tell him when they get home.

'You been making the pickups with these new people,' he says to Hector.

Hector nods.

Francisco goes into his delivery and throws a nice breaking ball, low and inside, for a called strike.

'You been doing anything else, Hector?'

Hector looks confused. 'What do you mean?'

Francisco sets up and Lado knows he's going to come with the fastball this time. Out in left field, Junior looks half asleep. Knows the ball isn't going to come his way. He's right, Lado thinks, but he needs to look sharper anyway.

'You're not double-dipping, are you?'

'No!'

It's the fastball, straight down the middle but

the kid's swing is behind it. Hector's a good man, been with them, what, six years? Never a problem, never any trouble.

'I wouldn't want anyone to think,' Lado says, 'that they can take advantage of these *gueros* just because they're new and a little soft. People need to know that they're under my protection.'

'Understood, Lado.'

You bet your brown Mexican ass, understood. If you're under Lado's umbrella no rain falls on you.

'Good,' Lado says. 'The next pickup needs to go smooth.'

'It will.'

Francisco wastes the next pitch, just like Lado knew he would. He's a smart kid, Francisco, up two in the count, no sense in wearing out his arm, throw the kid a bad pitch to see if he'll swing on it. Smart.

'How's your brother?' Lado asks. 'Antonio? He still selling cars?'

He can hear Hector's heart stop.

'Yes, he's fine, Lado. He'll be pleased you asked for him.'

'And his family? Two daughters, is it?'

'Yes. All well, *dio gracio.*'

Francisco goes into his windup. The stance is still too narrow, but the kid has that long whip arm so he gets away with it. Breaking ball that drops like it fell off a table and the batter swings and misses.

Two down.

And now Hector knows that if he's playing games with these *yerba* shipments he's dead, but not before his brother, sister-in-law, and nieces back in Tijuana.

'Delores! Hello!'

Lado turns to see Delores edging her way down the bench, saying hello to the other mothers. She sits down next to him.

'So *I'm* on time and *you're* late,' Lado says.

'I was waiting for the roof guys,' she says. 'Of course they came late.'

'I told you I'd take care of it.'

'Yes, but when?' she asks. 'It's supposed to be a wet winter. Has Junior batted yet?'

'Next inning probably.'

Francisco throws a low ball, pure junk, but the batter bites on it and pops up. Lado stands and claps as Francisco trots to the dugout, his glove folded casually under his arm.

'Let's take the boys to CPK after the game,' Lado says.

'Fine with me,' Delores says.

She can smell that hair-cutting whore on him.

The least he could do is take a shower.

170

She can smell him.
His sweat, his breath
As he comes toward her.

O twists her head away but

He stands right over, breathes into her face, stares

Into her face with those

Cold black eyes

She

Cries she

Chokes on her panic she

Can't turn it off.

Yeah, but you have to, girl, O tells herself.

She makes herself take a deep breath. Time to stop being girlie-girl about this. Time to cowgirl up, show some ovaries. She gets off the bed, walks to the door, and pounds on it.

'Yo!' she yells. 'I want Internet access!'

171

Yes, she wants fucking Internet.

She wants Internet, a computer to *use* the Internet, she's hoping like hell they have Wi-Fi wherever the fuck they are and not DSL or, God help them, *dial-up*. She wants all that plus she wants a TV, satellite TV – if I miss one more episode of *The Bachelorette* I'll never catch up – an iPod and access to her iTunes account, and could they mix in a *salad* every once in a while because if she keeps wolfing down these starches they'll need a forklift to get her out of here and deliver her to some fat farm in La Costa, which would make Paqu very happy and speaking of her mother . . .

'You want to let me use the Internet,' she says through the door, 'because if Moms doesn't hear from me every twenty-seven minutes she *will* call the FBI and I think but I'm not sure that one of my stepfathers – Four, maybe? – anyway, it doesn't matter, might have been in the FBI' – actually it was the FDIC but who fucking cares – 'so she *knows* people, and, oh yeah, I want to contact my friends to let them know I'm all right, or at least some version of all right, and would it kill you to whip up a martini?'

Esteban comes into her room.

He doesn't know what the fuck to say.

She snaps, 'Okay, what's your name?'

'Esteban.'

'Nice,' O says. 'Okay, Esteban, I want—'

She repeats her demands.

Esteban agrees to go ask.

172

This gets kicked all the way upstairs.

From the boys running the house where they have the girl stored, to Alex, to Lado, then to Elena.

Who buys the Paqu argument.

The last thing she wants is a 'hunt for the missing girl' drama all over American television, so she says, yes, provide the girl a computer and supervised use of the Internet. See that she writes her mother – make sure she gives no clues as to where

221

she really is – and let her write her friends, who are, after all, our business associates.

I already have one rebellious spoiled daughter, Elena thinks.

I need another one?

173

O writes Paqu:

Dear Mommy,

Hello from Paris, or should I say bonjour from Paree. It's very nice here, with the Eiffel Tower and all that. The pain au chocolat is awesome, but don't worry, I'm not eating too much. All the French women are very skinny, the bitches. Talk to you soon.

Your daughter,
Ophelia

The BC folks aren't idiots – they route the e-mail through one of their affiliates in France so the 'sent at' matches up.

Then O writes Chon and Ben:

Hi guys,

Get me the fugh outta here.

174

'They could just be writing it,' Chon says.
'No, it's her.'
'How do you know?'
'"Fugh"?'
They write back, 'We'll bring you back.'
Then try to figure out how to make that the truth.

175

Problem with that is
The BC have relocated all their stash houses.
Fun and games, fun and games but
It's the right move.
An ounce of prevention, pound o' cure. Lado and Elena put their heads together on it and made the call – new houses, new routes should solve the cash car prob for a little while, anyway, hopefully long enough to find the leak.
So Ben and Chon are screwed for targets. They staked out the stash houses in Dennis's files and all the occupants are gone. Just moved out and abandoned the places.
Here today, gone tomorrow, or
In Chon's experience
Hero today, gonzo tomorrow.

And while robbing themselves helps to throw off suspicion, you don't make any money robbing yourself. With uninsurable items like dope and dope money, anyway. ('Hello, State Farm? What would the premiums be on a ton of Sweet Dreams and – hello, State Farm?') Even that fucking gecko isn't going to go for that, ditto the Neanderthal guys.

And, anyway, you want to mix it up. It's the relentless cycle of guerrilla warfare, Chon knows. You act, the enemy adjusts. You adjust again, the enemy readjusts. And on and on and on.

'We could take them when they're coming *in* for a dope pickup,' Ben says, because he's, like, Butch Cassidy now. 'But we'd get that money anyway, so what's the point?'

'No point.'

But when they leave with the dope they just paid for . . .

Because dope is as good as money. Better, really, in this economy. Dope never slides against the euro.

So that's the new new plan they come up with: sell the BC the dope, then rob them of the dope you just sold them.

Because once it leaves the store . . .

176

Reagan and Ford.
A Republican robbery.
Ben flat out refuses to wear the Reagan mask

224

(for a half-ass Buddhist, Ben can hold a full-ass grudge) so Chon takes it. Ben puts on Ford and promptly bumps his head getting into the car.

'I'm a method hijacker,' Ben explains.

Chon doesn't approve of the levity.

'It could get ugly this time,' he warns.

'It's all fun and games until someone loses an eye,' Ben agrees.

177

They sit in a stolen Volvo station wagon half a mile from the grow house back out in Ortega country.

Yes, a Volvo station wagon.

'A Volvo?' Ben asked when Chon came back with the work car. 'Seriously?'

'These things are tanks.'

They handle for shit, but they crash beautifully.

So they sit in the Volvo and watch the BC van go in and then wait for the transaction to be completed and for the van to come back. There's only one road in so they know that the van will come back the same way, loaded with a shipment of primo Ultra.

'Your seat belt buckled?' Chon asks when they hear the van coming.

'Tray table locked and seat in an upright position.'

'Ramming speed.'

Because everyone loves *Animal House.*

They hit the van at a diagonal angle in the front

right quarter panel. Chon is out of the driver's seat before the car even stops. He shows the startled van driver the shotgun and jerks him out of the seat. Ben gets the drop on the rider. The driver is flat on the ground, Chon starts to get in and then—

Shit doesn't happen slo-mo the way it does in the movies.

It happens so freaking fast.

Sick fast:

Chon is hopping into the driver's seat when—

The shot goes off

So loud

The rest happens in silence, well,

Not *silence*, there's this weird sound of rushing water in Ben's ears as—

Chon spins and tumbles backward and Ben—

—screams, then

Starts shooting into the back of the van, and—

—the van door slides open and this guy tumbles out, bullet holes all over him as

Chon straightens up and fires the shotgun—

—and this guy slams back against the van like a crash-test dummy.

Chon pulls the body aside, gets behind the wheel. Ben jumps in and they head down the road.

178

Ben flips out.

'Easy,' Chon says. 'Steady.'

'I killed someone!'

226

'And thank fucking God,' Chon says.

The first shot had just missed him. The second would have killed him if Ben hadn't opened fire. He looks over at Ben, tears pouring down his cheeks, his face twisted in pain.

Brings it back. The first time.

Popping that particular cherry.

No time for guilt then.

AQ all over the fucking place. Sniper fire coming from everywhere. Buddies going down to the *zip-zip* of bullets. Chon, flat on the ground, forced himself to look up, find a target, fire.

You killed one, pup? Kill more. Now he tells Ben, 'Chill.'

'I can't.'

'What did you think it was going to be, Ben?' And don't you know it's going to get worse?

179

Focus, focus, Ben demands of himself. Focus on saving O.

With one of theirs killed, the BC will feel obligated to Do Something About It and they might do it to O if they suspect our involvement in the robbery.

Gotta give them someone else.

It's too bad, the dope is mid-six figures but they have to dump it. Dump the dope and their guilt onto Somebody Else.

It's ugly, it's wrong, and—

They drive the van to Dana Point.

DP is a funky old surf town that has retained some of its funk. It used to be famous among surfers as 'Killer Dana' for a big wave that crashed right onto the point of Dana Point. But then they built the harbor and the marina and fucked up the wave. All that's left of Killer Dana is an eponymous—

—good word, Chon has postulated that
Alcoholics Anonymous is also
Alcoholics Eponymous—

—surf shop that maintains the legend, anyway.

Dana Point also has a small but distinct barrio with a small but growing gang problem. Ben has it in mind to give the small but growing gang problem a bigger problem. Chon pulls the van into the barrio, finds a nice little cul-de-sac, and leaves it there.

He and Ben walk.

180

On the walk Ben conducts an internal Socratic self-cross-examination.

You took a human life.

Yes, but in self-defense.

Not really, you were robbing him, he was the one defending himself.

Actually, he was robbing me first.

So two wrongs make a right?

Of course they don't, but when he pulled the gun he left me no choice.

228

Certainly he did. Would it not have been the moral choice to allow him to kill you instead of committing a murder yourself?

I guess, but I just reacted.

Exactly. You didn't think.

There wasn't time to think. Only react.

But you put yourself in that situation. You committed a robbery, you carried a gun. Those were choices.

He would have killed me.

Now you are merely repeating yourself.

He would have killed my friends.

So you were saving them, not yourself?

I don't know what the hell I was doing, all right?! I don't recognize myself. I don't know who I am anymore.

And it's all fun and games until someone loses an I.

181

When the dope van didn't arrive Hector and his boys drove the route and found two of their men sitting beside a body in the road.

Gun still in his hand.

Lado had him carefully wrapped in sheets of canvas and put respectfully in the back of the truck.

'Bury him like a man,' he ordered. 'He died doing his job. Money to his family.'

Then he went off to find the killers.

Two DP wannabe gangbangers spotted the strange van and took about fifteen seconds to boost it.

Joyrode it down to Doheny Beach, where they looked in the back and couldn't believe their luck.

All that *yerba.*

Wide-eyed, Sal looks at Jumpy and asks, 'How much you think this is worth?'

'Lots.'

Mucho dinero.

They can't help but sample just a little. Peel a corner of the wrapping off one brick—

'Is that blood, *hermano?*'

'*Mierdita,* is that hair?'

—and smoke up.

Unreal, *cabron.*

A one-toke high but they each take three. Inside five minutes they're higher than the sky.

'We're rich,' Jumpy says.

'Where can we sell it?' Sal asks.

'This shit?' Jumpy says. 'Anywhere.'

They bliss out on this thought for a few minutes, then Sal really fires up. 'Think for a second,' he says, although this is very difficult. 'This could be our ticket.'

They been trying to break in for a while. This could be that stamp on the hand that lets them in and out of the club.

VIP Room, too.

Ben and Chon go back to the house because it would look suspicious not to.

'If we don't go back,' Ben reasons, 'we can never go back. They'll know it's us.'

So they go back to Table Rock, but gun up for the expected invasion. Shotguns, pistols, rifles, machine guns – Chon's whole arsenal is at the ready. But even the Mexicans aren't going to come to a beach house in Laguna in the middle of the day for a shootout.

If they want us, Chon knows, they'll wait.

At least until night.

More likely they'll be more patient than that. Send the pros to wait it out, pick them off as opportunity presents itself.

As it would, as it will.

They don't get an invasion, they get a text.

Summoning Ben to a sit-down.

Come alone.

'They're going to grab you,' Chon says.

'Or hit me on the way there or back,' Ben says.

'I doubt it,' Chon offers. 'They'd want to torture you first. Probably tape it so they can teach a lesson.'

'Thanks.'

But he goes.

The other way with it.

Takes the offensive.

He meets Lado and Alex at a public place, the boardwalk at Town Beach, gets the news about the bloody jacking and the insinuation of guilt and he goes off.

'You better fucking do something about this,' Ben says to Lado. 'I've been in this business for eight years and never had a person as much as scratched. I hook up with you and I get robbed, and now you're telling me a man is dead?!'

'Take it—'

'*You* take it easy,' Ben says, jabbing Alex in the chest. 'I thought you were the fucking Baja Cartel. I thought you offered protection. Well, it looks like you may be pretty good at snatching girls off the street, but when it comes to—'

'Enough.' This from Lado.

Ben shuts his mouth but shakes his head and walks ahead of him.

Nice day on Town Beach.

People in the water.

Sleek, tall, cut women playing volleyball. The muscles of their bare abs tight as drums.

The boys are out on the b-ball court. Middle-age gay men watch from the benches.

Sun shining on it all.

Another day in paradise.

Alex catches up with him. 'You're saying you had nothing to do with this.'

'I'm saying,' Ben, well, says, 'that I'm going to have nothing to do with *you* if this keeps up. Deal or no deal, I'm not putting my people in harm's way. You want my product, you guarantee our safety or I'm shutting it down. And you can call the Queen and tell her that. Better yet, put me on the phone, I'll tell her that.'

'I don't think you want to do that, Ben,' Alex says. 'Remember who—'

'Yeah, I remember,' Ben says, making a point to look at Lado. 'And as for your fucking aspersions, your asinine accusations that we're somehow in on this shit, fuck you and the goat you rode in on. I'm not putting up with any more of that, either.'

'You'll put up with what we tell you to put up with,' Lado says.

'Just handle your own problems, okay?' Ben says. 'Don't worry about me. I'm taking care of business.'

He walks away.

Crosses the PCH and leaves them standing there.

185

Sal comes to Jesus.

Yeah, it's a cheap joke, but what do you want, it's his name.

233

They find Jesus where you always find him, in the parking lot behind the liquor store, next to the car wash, hanging with five other 94s, drinking beer and smoking a little *yerba*.

Eleven AM and they're just out.

Three years now, Sal and Jumpy been trying to join the 94, but been shut out. Jesus told them it wasn't like the old days – you lived in the barrio, you could get jumped in – now you have to bring something to the table, *m'ijo, ese*. You have to bring – what did Jesus call it? Assets.

'Hola, Jesus.'

Hola, hola, m'ijo, all that.

186

Jesus is no kid anymore.

He's twenty-three, and he's spent eight of those twenty-three behind bars. Lucky not to have spent more, all the gangbanging he did. Him and the other 94s, defending their turf against the other Mexican gangs.

Cliché, stereotyped you've-seen-it-all-in-the-movies drive-by, eye-for-an-eye bullshit. By age twelve Jesus already had a sheet. Beat the fuck out of another kid, the judge looked at those unrepentant eyes (remorse? for *what*?) and sent him to the CYA in Vista, where the bigger boys made him jack them off and suck their dicks until he got more angry than scared and grabbed one of them by the hair and slammed his head into

234

the concrete wall until it looked like a sloppy tagging.

Came out, got beat into the 94s (again, cliché, stereotyped you've-seen-it-all-in-the-movies), thirteen years old selling dope on the corner, fucking fourteen-year-old *chucha* on bare mattresses in crack houses, gets caught with the crack in his hand, don't give up nobody and he's back in CYA, but this time he *is* one of the bigger boys (got thick forearms, big hands, some weight on him) and it's him who makes the smaller boys jerk him off, suck his cock, and he looks at them with those dead eyes and they do it, do what he says.

Out again, the gang wars are on, they just shoot the shit out of each other for drug turf, for revenge, for fucking nothing, he takes a bullet in a drive-by. Just hanging out on the front lawn, smoking *yerba,* drinking cerveza, getting ready to tip his *piton* into this sweet little piece when *bam* he feels this pain in his thigh and the piece is screaming but not like he likes her to and there's blood running down his leg. He finishes his beer before he goes to the hospital.

When he goes out two weeks later, still with a cane, to get a little of his own back, he has his boys drive him past a house in the Los Treintes barrio, sticks his AK out the window, and lets loose. Gets a Treinte but also gets a four-year-old *niña* on the rebound, but Jesus don't care about that.

The *prole* don't get him for that, but they're laying for him because now he's a *jefe* and they're looking to put him away. He fucks up and gives them their shot, too. This *lambioso* takes a long look at his girl and Jesus just goes off and smashes the guy's face and they put him away for six in the Q.

Except for the food and the lack of *chucha*, Jesus liked prison.

Pumping iron, hanging with the same boys he'd hang with on the corner, fighting the Aryans and the Zulus, blowing *yerba*, skinpopping, fucking punks, getting tatts. He killed two more men in the Q and they never got near him for it. No one was going to talk on Jesus. Ran the 94s, or what was left of them, from his cell. Ordered three more killings on the street and they got done, too.

Out again, back again to the 94s and found there wasn't much left of them. A lot of them were dead, more in the joint, some were *craquedos* and junkies. The gangbanging thing was over, *finito*.

And he ain't that young anymore.

The years, they slide.

The people, they don't.

The people, they grind and scrape and it shows.

Anyway, he did his time and now he's out and now he's back and they say the days of the gangs are over, we all killed each other off and there's some truth in that but there's some false in it, too. The gangs are coming back – like they say, good taste never goes out of style – but in a different way.

A serious way.

A business way.

Making money.

The prison counselors used to yap about 'making good choices.' Make good choices when you get out so you don't come back in.

Good choices.

So you can choose to kill for pride, for some silly-ass gang colors, for territory, for drug turf, or you can choose to kill for money.

Jesus chooses to kill for money.

Like the saying goes, 'Do something that you love for a living, and you'll never work a day in your life.'

187

'What can I do for you boys?' Jesus asks.

Jesus is the *jefe* of the 94s, got them a little *plaza* in DP, looking to move into the big Mexican hood in the SJC.

But the SJC is Treinte country, so Jesus looks elsewhere for support. Has made him the big hookup with a rep of EL Azul himself, because everyone knows that he's going to come out on top, and then Jesus looks to move up with the winner. Perform for EL Azul, and when he takes over, he'll give SJC to the 94.

Sal tries to play it strong. 'It's what we can do for each other.'

Jesus laughs. '*Bueno, m'ijo,* what can we do for each other?'

Sal turns and waves to Jumpy, who pulls the van up.

'I don't do cars,' Jesus says.

Not worth the risk, not worth the aggra. You steal a car, you drive all the way down to Mexico, and then they rob you on the price.

'Look inside.'

Sal opens the passenger door and beckons.

'What you *niños* got in there,' Jesus smirks. 'TV sets?'

Nooooo, not TV sets.

Assets.

Jesus whistles. 'Where did you get this?'

Sal is pleased with the reaction. Not easy to impress Jesus. 'Let's just say we got it,' he says, pointing his first and index fingers like a *pistola.*

'I hope you dumped the hardware,' Jesus says.

Which is very good, because now they're talking between men.

'Can you help us sell it?' Jumpy asks.

'For a taste,' Sal quickly adds.

Sure, Jesus answers. He can do that.

There has to be a good 200K in that van. Kick some of that up to El Azul and he gets his attention. He turns to one of his boys and says, 'Get my cousins here some beers.'

Sal is happy.

Stands and drinks beer in the VIP Room.

Jesus goes to see a man he knows.

Who will be very happy to buy this merchandise at a good price.

Antonio Machado owns five taco stands in South Orange County, a good cash business to own, because he moves a lot more dope than chimichangas.

Jesus chose Señor Machado because the man has ties with El Azul. The *jefe* will get his kick-up, Jesus will make Machado look good and get favors in return, and they'll all make a lot of money. Even better, Machado is happy to lowball his offer to Sal and Jumpy, then pay Jesus the real amount, which will cover his kick to both Machado and El Azul.

It's good, smart business.

Would be, anyway, except—

Jesus lacks a vital piece of information.

Señor Machado has seen certain video clips. He's had visits from Lado, who explained to him that he should know which side his tortilla is buttered on, and this El Azul business? Don't lose your head over that.

The Queen lives, *Tio*.

Long live the Queen.

And he's also received, just this morning, an Amber Alert on a certain shipment of marijuana that suffered a misfortune: in no uncertain terms, our good friend Antonio, anyone who moves that *yerba* puts his own *cabeza* on the block. Anyone who sees or even hears about that *yerba* and doesn't pick up a phone . . .

Machado picks up the phone.

Goes out in back of one of his stores, where the counter is busy with schoolchildren coming to visit the Mission, and he makes the call.

'You're a good friend,' Lado says. 'We knew we could count on you.'

Set up the sale.

189

Jesus squirms in the fishing net suspended from the beam.

'I'm going to ask you again,' Lado says. 'Where did you get this *yerba*?'

'From those two,' Jesus says, pointing down to Sal and Jumpy, who sit propped against the wall.

'From those two *perritos*?' Hernan asks, jutting his chin toward the two boys, who sit in a pool of their own piss. 'I don't think so. Try again.'

'I did!' It comes out as a whine.

Lado shakes his head and swings the bat. Big baseball fan, Lado. Thought at one point he might have a crack at the pros. A cup of coffee in Double A, maybe. Now he loves to go to Padres games. Gets there early to watch batting practice.

Jesus screams.

'That was a single,' Lado says. 'This is going to be a double off the left field wall.'

He swings again.

Jumpy hears a bone break and starts to cry.

Again.

'You want a triple?' Lado says. 'Tell me the truth. Tell me *enough* truth I might let you live.'

Jesus breaks down. 'It was me, I did it.'

Lado, a little winded, leans on the bat. 'Not alone, you didn't. Who are you with?'

'The Nine-Four.'

'Never heard of them. What's that?'

'My gang.'

'Your "gang,"' Lado says. 'You little balls of shit couldn't pull off a *tombe* like this. Who do you answer to?'

'The Baja Cartel.'

'*Pendejo, I'm* the Baja Cartel.'

'The other one.'

'What one?'

'El Azul.'

Lado nods. 'And who with El Azul told you where to be and when?'

Jesus doesn't have an answer.

He really doesn't.

Not even when Lado hits a triple.

Not even when he hits a grand slam.

Jesus just spits out a lot of incoherent shit. This guy came to see him, he doesn't know the guy's name, the mystery man gave him the info about the dope run, suggested he should hit it, they'd split the profits . . .

'Do you know a man named Ben?' Lado asks. 'Was it him?'

Jesus is happy for any suggestions. 'Yes, that was it, Ben.'

'What did Ben look like?'

Wrong answers, wrong answers. Jesus can't describe Ben, he can't describe Chon.

Fregado – useless.

'Would these know?' Lado asks, pointing to Sal and Jumpy.

Yes, Jesus tells him, they'd know.

190

Sal whimpers.

He can smell his own fear, his own filth.

Can't stop his legs from shaking or the tears pouring out his eyes or the snot running out his nose.

Jesus's moans have stopped.

He lies like a pile of dirty clothes.

Lado puts his pistol to Jumpy's forehead and shoots, splattering pieces of Sal's friend all over him. Then he turns to Sal and asks, 'Do you really expect me to believe that you just found a van full of *yerba* parked in your barrio and you took it? Is that what you expect me to believe?'

'I don't know.'

Lado puts the gun to his head.

191

The photo comes across Ben's screen.
Three dead kids
With the legend—
'taking care of business.'

192

O sits on her bed and watches an episode of
The Bachelorette on Hulu.

'I'm telling you,' Esteban says, 'she's going for
the wrong guy. That boy there is a *player.*'

O disagrees. 'I think he's sweet, and vulnerable.'

Esteban don't know what 'vulnerable' means but
he knows what a player is, and that boy in the hot
tub there is a *player.*

Maybe maybe, O thinks.

Men know men.

She and Esteban have formed a nice little relationship. He's her new BFF. Sure, probably a case
of Stockholm syndrome (O saw this thing on TV
once about Patty Hearst), and he's no Ashley, but
he seems like a nice kid. So in *love* with his fiancée,
OMG is the boy whipped. He tells O all about
Lourdes and the baby, and she gives him sage,
sisterly advice on how to treat a woman.

'Jewelry is very important,' she tells him. 'Jewelry
and lotion. I'd pull back on the chocolates, though,
because she's probably feeling all fat and stuff.'

'She is.' Esteban sighs.

'Yeah, well, *you* didn't bag the groceries, *amigo*,' O says. 'And are you doing the deed regularly?'

'*Que?*'

'Drilling for oil, digging for gold, performing your husbandly duties?' O forms a 'V' with two fingers of her left hand and shoves her right index finger back and forth between them.

Esteban is shocked. 'She's pregnant!'

'Not dead,' O says. 'And during her second trimester her hormones are hopping around like bunnies in a field of clover. She's hornier than a convent. You have to take care of business, boyfriend, or she'll think *you* don't think she's beautiful anymore, and then look out.'

'She is beautiful.' Esteban sighs.

Whipped, whipped, whipped.

'Show her.'

Actually, one of the things O likes about Esteban is that he's sexually unthreatening.

Which O appreciates these days.

She doesn't really like the idea of being touched, never mind being entered, being *violated,* which she used to like a lot. Her once voracious sexual appetite has dwindled to a sensual bulimia. Her little bud that used to pop out and welcome any new sensation now hides in the closet in the fetal position.

Thank you so much, my clit-sis, Elena.

And Chain Saw Guy.

Summoning that image is a mistake because it turns on the vid-clip. She squeezes her eyes shut and when she opens them again the bachelor's head is floating in water and it's a second before she realizes that he's just sunk down in the hot tub, but for a second there it sure looked like the bachelorette was bobbing for apples.

'Stebo, you got any weed?'

'I'm not supposed to . . .'

'Come on.'

Show some *huevos*.

193

'We did this,' Ben says, looking at the images.

'Lado did it,' Chon answers.

'We caused it,' Ben says.

Chon goes off. Rare rush of valuable words. 'If you're going to wallow in this self-indulgent guilt trip you should never have started this in the first place. What do you think happens in a war? You think only soldiers get killed?

'You knew what you were doing when you left that van in the hood. You knew you were setting a trap. Don't be so hypocritical as to now feel sorry for the bait.

'And you know it's not going to stop here. Azul's people will have to respond. There'll be more dead kids within days. Then a counterresponse, then a counter-counter until it's Gandhi's world of the blind. But isn't that what we started out to do?'

Chon knows what war is.

What it turns us into.

They know that Lado will keep going.

He believes there is a leak in his organization, a turncoat working for Azul, and he won't stop until he finds him.

'Or we feed him one,' Ben says.

194

At goddamn last.

Party City in Irvine, Deputy Berlinger talks to a stoner clerk who remembers selling a Letterman and a Leno mask.

'You remember the guy?'

'Sort of.'

Sort of.

Fucking blazers.

'Can you describe him for me?' Amazingly, the kid can.

Tall white guy. Brown eyes, brown hair, didn't say much.

Paid cash.

Something, anyway, Berlinger thinks.

To get Alex off my aching ass.

195

You put Spin (the Money Washer) together with Jeff and Craig (the Computer Geeks) and you have:

246

(A) The Three Stooges

(B) The Three Tenors

(C) A Trio that Can Hack into Bank Accounts and Make $ Appear Anywhere

If you guessed (C), you win. What these boys do – at Ben's direction – is find Alex Martinez's American bank account, then create a new one for him, transfer deposits of thirty, forty-five, and thirty-three thousand dollars into it, spin it around the world a few times, and wash it back into new accounts.

Then they buy him a condo in Cabo.

Then they goof around some more and launder all this through several DBAs and holding companies so that only a skilled forensic accountant could understand it.

196

Jaime is a skilled forensic accountant.

He and Ben sit in a booth at the bar in the St Regis.

'What do you want?' Jaime asks.

'Uncomfortable?' Ben responds. 'I know you and Alex usually come to these meetings together. You're like Mormon missionaries, the two of you. All you need is the white shirts and the skinny black ties.'

'So why did you want to meet me alone?'

Ben says, 'I had my people do a little research.'

He slides a folder of documents over to Jaime, who looks at it like it's some foreign object from outer space.

'Open it,' Ben says.

Jaime opens the file. Starts looking at it and then can't stop. Starts turning pages faster and faster, flipping back and forth, his face bent closer to the file, his finger tracing lines and columns.

This stuff, Ben thinks, is like porn to an accountant.

Yeah, sort of, but not really. Jaime and Alex are boys, and when the former finally looks up his face is ashen.

He is seriously bummed. Ben bums him more. Cranks up the dial on the bum-meter. 'Check the deposit dates, match them up with the hijackings, and then try to tell yourself that our little Alex isn't getting rich off my dope.'

'Where did you get this?'

'I got it,' Ben says. 'But run it again yourself. By all means, check my homework.'

'I will,' Jaime says. 'Alex has a wife and three kids. I'm god-father to his oldest daughter.'

'You have kids of your own?'

'Two boys. Eight and six.'

'Well,' Ben says, 'you're the accountant on this and it happened on your watch. Knowing the temperament of your client, I'd say it's either his kids grow up without a daddy, or yours do. Unless . . . oh, J, you're not in on this *with* him, are you?'

Ben leaves a twenty and Jaime sitting there.

197

Alex gets summoned to a meeting with Lado. Alex gets:

(A) A bonus
(B) A promotion
(C) A strong talking-to
(D)

If you guessed (D) . . .

198

Alex can't explain
The source of his income.
The three deposits, the condo.
It's like a *really* bad meeting with an IRS auditor, except Alex can't bring in H&R Block or any of those gunners that advertise on the radio.

He has to be his own attorney, but he doesn't have the right to remain silent. And it ain't no police interview room, it's a warehouse out in the flats of Costa Mesa. At least Alex isn't dangling from the ceiling, Lado knows his man – the lawyer isn't tough, there's no need for the piñata routine. So he just has Alex tied hand and foot, and he slaps him around a little, that's all.

The *lambioso* lawyer is already crying.

Chon and Ben have been summoned to the meeting, too.

Elena's idea.
To see how they react.
Ben watches this movie in horror.

CUT TO:

199

INT. WAREHOUSE – NIGHT

ALEX sits propped against a wall. Blood trickles from his mouth and flecks of blood spatter the shoulders of his gray Armani suit.

LADO squats beside him, speaking quietly.

LADO
Who paid you?

ALEX
Nobody.

LADO
Azul? 94?

ALEX
I swear to God. No one.

LADO
Look, you're going to die. We both know this. But I like you and you have given years of good

service. So I'm going to give you this chance. You can die – or you and your whole family can die.

ALEX starts to sob.

LADO (CONT.)
Tell me the truth – right now – and your wife and kids cash in your insurance policy. Lie to me again and I'll go to your house, tell them you've been in an accident, and bring them here. I'll kill them in front of you.

200

Ben can't breathe.

The world spins and he thinks he might throw up, but he can feel Chon willing.

Not one word. Not one goddamn word.

Alex straightens up, swallows, looks Lado in the eyes, and says, 'It was Azul. He's using the 94.'

Lado pats him on the head and stands up.

Takes a revolver out of his belt and

Hands it to Ben.

'Do it.'

201

'He took *your* money, too,' Lado says reasonably, 'so you should do him. My gift to you.'

'I'll do it,' Chon says.

'I said *him,* not *you,*' Lado snaps.

He looks into Ben's eyes.

As he presses the pistol into Ben's hand.

Do it, Chon wills.

You have to do it. Think about O.

Ben shoots twice

into Alex's chest.

202

'So it was Alex,' Ben says out in the parking lot.

His hand shakes like a haunted house skeleton.

'It was Alex,' Lado agrees.

'We're in the clear.'

A terse nod.

'Then it's business as usual?'

Sí, Business As Usual.

'I want to Skype O.'

Lado thinks about that for a second, then agrees.

203

O's face

Lights up when she sees them

Big smile. 'Hi, guys!'

Hi.

Hi.

'How are you?' Ben asks, feeling stupid.

'You know, I'm okay,' O says. 'It's a slacker girl's fantasy – I'm actually forced at gunpoint to lie around my room and do nothing but watch bad TV.'

'It won't be for much longer.'

'No?'

'No.'

'How are you guys?'

'Yeah, good,' Chon says.

'Ben, you good?'

'Yeah, I'm fine,' Ben says.

The session is cut off.

204

Yeah, Ben's fine.

205

'Did you notice the background on the Skype?' Ben asks Chon. 'It's a different place.'

He's watched it about thirty times.

'And listen . . .'

He jacks the volume up. 'What's that in the background?'

'Voices.'

'Speaking . . .'

'English.'

206

Danny Benoit is a deacon in the Church of the Lighter Day Saints.

And a highly paid sound technician who makes the 405 run from his home in Laguna Canyon up to the L.A. recording studios about once a month in a '66 Vette he calls the Pirate Ship.

'I sail it up to L.A. once a month,' Danny says, 'fill it full of loot, and sail it back before I get caught.'

Danny B is gold.

Or platinum.

DB can make an average voice great and a great voice sublime. 'The biggest names in the recording industry' all want Danny on the mixer.

He could give a shit who they are.

He ain't interested in dropping names

Rubbing elbows

Hanging out

He just wants to do his mix, make his money, and come home.

And Danny does some of his best work for Ben & Chonny's.

They've been known to give him mixes depending on what 'artist' he's sweetening at the moment. He wants *sativa* for the hip-hop, *indica* for R&B? Say the word, my man, and B&C will shortcut the usual distribution network and have it delivered direct.

Ben likes hearing tunes on the radio and knowing he contributed.

'They should put your names on the CDs,' Danny said once. In fact, he was going to thank them at the Grammys one night but fortunately thought better of it.

It would have been cool, but, uncool.

They take a recording of the Skype session to him at his house. Danny looks like your basic hippie who knows that the seventies are way over but doesn't care. T-shirt, jeans, sandals, ponytail.

It's rude to come to someone's house empty-handed so they bring him a bag of Moon Landing. ('Some say it happened, some say it was staged, we say who gives a fuck.') Danny has immaculate stoner manners and offers it around.

Formalities over, Ben asks, 'Can you enhance this?'

'Can Kobe drain a three?'

He puts it on his home system, dials some dials, switches some switches back and forth, and in a minute you might as well have been in the room with O. And the English speakers in the background?

'Radio,' Danny pronounces. 'FM.'

'American station?'

Danny has a very fine ear. He knows his stations from frequent listening to find out who's ripping him on royalties. (The answer, of course, is that everyone is – it's that kind of business. Drugs, movies, music – all a circle-jerk of larceny.) He can listen to empty air and know which station it is.

'KROC,' he says after listening to it a few times. '"The Kroc on your dial." Out of L.A. Enchilada plate of current pop hits and nineties music.'

'O listens to it,' Chon says.

'Can it reach Mexico?'

'It can,' Danny says, 'but not with this clarity. This signal is beautiful.'

Yes it is, Ben thinks.

207

Back to the file, back to research.

If they have O in Southern California, where?

It takes a lot of digging, but they hit on it.

Dennis has 'concerns' about a company called Gold Coast Realty, based in . . . wait for it . . .

Laguna Beach, CA.

'Gold Coast Realty,' Ben says. 'Ring a bell?'

'Didn't you buy *this* house from GCR?'

'Yeh.'

'Steve Ciprian.'

Steve Ciprian, owner of Gold Coast.

Charter member of the Church of the Lighter Day Saints.

Aka Stepdad Six.

208

Steve is not hard to find.

You can locate him at:

(A) The bar at the Ritz-Carlton
(B) The bar at the St Regis
(C) The golf course

Steve freely admits to being a high-functioning alcoholic. High-functioning because he drinks only martinis at the bars and (expensive) wine over dinner, gets away with wearing only aloha shirts and khaki slacks, spends his nondrinking time playing tennis and golf and cheating on whichever wife he's currently on, smokes dope, and makes about a gazillion dollars a year selling the most exclusive homes on the Gold Coast – that stretch off the PCH between Dana Point and Newport Beach.

Yeah, he used to make that much a year, anyway, before the Crash. Now everyone is trying to sell but no one is able to buy, and Steve is trying to ride it out by whittling down his handicap while dodging phone calls.

And blazing up more.

Been a tough year for Steve.

Business goes in the shitter.

His secretary threatens to tell his wife about them.

His wife throws him out anyway for reasons having nothing to do with his banging his secretary but because he couldn't get enthused about her wanting to become a 'life coach,' whatever the fuck that is.

A bummer, having to relocate, but Kim was fast approaching her 'sell by' date anyway, and looking on the bright side, there are a dozen houses in foreclosure that he can move in to for the time being. It will shut his secretary up until he dumps her ass and then cans her, and

The secretary is a mouthy pain in the ass, but what a rack.

He's sitting at the bar at the St Regis starting in on the second martini when Ben and Chon come in.

Always a pleasure to see them.

Good times, those boys.

To watch them play volleyball was to watch the storied poetry in motion, to smoke their dope a touch of the sublime, and Steve can't remember which one of them was tapping Kim's whack-job but tasty little daughter.

Christ, he wouldn't have minded mooring his boat in that tight little slip, but the chick never gave him as much as a second look.

Too bad.

A little mother-daughter action.

And the kid had a funny name for Kim she let drop when they were both really high one night, when he thought he saw a sliver of an opening with her, what was it she called her?

That's right – 'Paqu.'

Passive Aggressive Queen of the Universe.

She got that right, and now the uppity bitch has found Jesus. Good – let Jesus pay for her next eye tuck.

Ben and Chon come sit next to him.

One on each side.

'Steve,' Ben says.

That's it, just Steve.

'Ben. Chon.'

'Steve.'

'Well, we got our names down,' Steve says.

'I have a name for you,' Ben says.

Elena Sanchez Lauter.

'Get the fuck out of here.'

No, he means—

Get the fuck out of here.

209

They take it to Steve's office.

They take it to Steve's office because that's where Chon suggests they take it and he looks like he wants what he wants. He also wants Steve's secretary to take an early day. So she takes her luscious boobs and goes.

Steve says, 'Guys, maybe you don't know what you're messing with here.'

'You've been buying property for Elena Sanchez and the Baja Cartel,' Ben says. 'Under shell names, DBAs, whatever.'

'Come on, guys.'

'I want a list.'

'You want a list.'

'What I just said, Steve.'

'Even if I did what you said, which I'm not saying I did,' Steve whines, 'and even if I had such a list, which I'm not saying I do, you have any idea what could happen to me if I let that information out?'

Chon is no mood to argue. 'You have any idea what could happen to you if you don't?'

He grabs Steve by the throat and lifts him up with one hand.

'This is for your stepdaughter, piece of shit,' Chon says. 'You give me that list or I'll kill you right now.'

They leave with the list.

210

Houses, condos, ranches.

They check listing after listing.

It all tells a story – Elena La Reina has been steadily buying up properties in Southern California. And not flipping them, either. They're all over God's little acre. Laguna, Laguna Niguel, Dana Point, Mission Viejo, Irvine, Del Mar.

'They wouldn't have taken her to the burbs,' Chon says.

So the ranches.

Mostly down in San Diego County.

Rancho Santa Fe—

'Too toney, too crowded.' Ramona, Julian.

'More isolated up in those hills. Possible.'

Anza-Borrego.

Vast, mostly empty desert.

Elena's bought three properties out there, several hundred acres each.

'What the fuck for?' Chon asks. 'Stash houses?'

Ben shrugs.

The phone rings and it's Jaime. Staff meeting.

O gets (Esteban-supervised) full use of the Internet. She can go online and surf. She can watch movies and television. They open the back door and Esteban takes her on daily walks around a walled-in garden and O can see that they're in the desert somewhere.

They even let Esteban send out for pizza.

212

It's a yeeee-had.

Full-out war between Treinte and 94, a surrogate battle shadowing the struggle between Elena and El Azul South of the Border down Mexico way.

It had to happen. Just a matter of time, all the experts say, a little gratified to see their gloomiest prognostications realized. The drug violence in Mexico *had* to leak across the border. A pool of blood seeping under the fence, an unstoppable toxic tide like the *mujados* coming across.

Like—

The Swine Flu.

(Except you won't need a 'pre-existing medical condition' and there is no vaccine.)

Heche en Mexico.

Drug war.

Treinte strikes back at 94. Then 94 strikes back

at Treinte. The bodies start stacking up in the barrios of SoCal. It will only be a matter of time, the grave newscasters warn, before an innocent (white) person gets killed.

'Why is this my problem?' Ben asks Jaime at the 'staff meeting,' which takes place in the parking lot at Salt Creek Beach.

'From now on, you deliver your product to us,' Jaime tells Ben.

'No way,' Ben says. 'I'm not putting my people at risk.'

'There's no risk,' Jaime says. 'We plugged the leak.'

Yeah. Ben remembers 'plugging the leak.' Ben sees it over and over again, his hand pulling the trigger on Alex. Now he says, 'I don't know . . .'

'There's no argument,' Jaime says.

Putting a Lid (as it were) on It

That's our decision.

Well, then—

213

EXT. BEN'S HOUSE – THE DECK – DAY

BEN and CHON stand at the railing and look off at the cerulean blue ocean.

CHON

We'll know where their stash houses are.

BEN

We will know where their stash houses are, yes.

BEN lights a bowl of dope and takes a hit.

CHON

Lot of money in a stash house.

BEN

Hence the name 'stash house.'

CHON

We could kick this to a whole new level. We could make the rest of the money with one big score.

BEN passes the pipe to CHON.

BEN

We could.

CUT TO:

214

Yeah, they *could* – doesn't mean they *should*.
What they probably should do is realize that they've been very lucky and gotten away with a whole lot of shit that they shouldn't have gotten away with, that's what they probably should do.
They *should* – doesn't mean they *will*.

It's the baditude.

'It will be bloody,' Chon says.

Ben doesn't care anymore.

One big score.

Irresistible.

It's been six weeks since they took her, and now they're one last big score from getting O back. From ending this nightmare. (Sure, but can he end the night*mares*? He doesn't know.) From getting the hell out of the hell and starting a new life.

Pull this off, get away with it, they're free and clear.

If people get hurt, they get hurt, Ben thinks. And a lot fewer people will probably get hurt if they hit a car than if they hit the house where they have O, even if they can find it. And these motherfuckers? After what they did to those three kids? And Alex? And O? After what they've turned me into?

Fuck 'em.

But be honest. You turned yourself into what you are now.

Okay, so fuck me.

Fuck 'em.

Okay, but how?

It's the Wild West out there with the BC Civil War raging north of the border.

So new regs on all shipments – cash, dope, or both.

Lado's Rules:

Three cars – the cargo car, one in front, one in back. All porcupines, bristling with guns and gunmen.

So how you gonna beat that?

They used to call it 'guerrilla warfare,' now they call it something else – 'non-symmetrical conflict.'

You gotta love guys who can come up with language like that.

Non-symmetrical conflict.

Different name, same thing.

The small versus the big.

217

Your strengths are your weaknesses.

The more you try to protect something, the more vulnerable you make it.

To wit:

Lado pulls his stash houses from the suburbs to rural locations that he can protect.

Makes fewer cash runs with more protection.

They go in the day instead of at night.

Fine but

Rural means isolated.

Fewer runs mean more cash per run, and day means

Chon doesn't have to buy a nightscope.

And they know where the concentrated stash houses are, so it's just a matter of surveillance to know when and where the cash convoys are going to roll out.

Knowing is one thing.

Doing another.

'We're going to need more ordnance,' Chon tells Ben after literally scoping out the stash house in the desert.

Fine, Ben says.

218

Chon rides the pony down to Calexico, right on the border.

Etymology obvious:

California

Mexico

Calexico.

The name reflects the reality. You take a walk in old downtown Calexico you aren't sure which country you're in. Truth is, you're in neither and both.

Chon goes to see this man he knows. You meet some interesting people around the edges of the elite forces thing. Guys who dig the scene, probably a little too much, for a lot of different reasons. And probably more of these guys cluster around the border, again for a whole lot of reasons.

Some of them see themselves as Davy Crockett.

Except this time they keep the Alamo.

You look at Barney, you don't think elite forces. You think pudgy Smurf with bottle glasses, bad breath, and lung cancer.

Anyway, Barney is happy to see Chon.

'What can I do you for?'

'A Barrett.'

That is, a Barrett Model 90. A humongoid sniper rifle that can send a .50-cal bullet into a target with accuracy from a mile away.

'Jesus, who are you going to shoot with that?' Barney asks.

'Cans,' Chon answers truthfully.

'My *man*,' Barney says.

Yeah, it's that kind of world.

Chon buys the Barrett and a 10X Leupold M-type scope to go with it.

219

O writes Paqu:

Dear Mommy,

Rome is GR8. The Colisiam is awesome. Everyone rides around on motor scooters and the men are beautiful. So are the women. So is the food. I mean, you think you've had pasta until you've been here, but you haven't. (Don't worry, I'm not eating too much of it.)

I miss you.

How RU?

Ophelia

220

Ben goes to Home Depot, Radio Shack, and HobbyTown USA.
With Chon's shopping list.
Because . . .

221

Chon's going Sunni on them.
IED.
You don't have bombers, missiles, and drones, so you come up with Improvised Explosive Devices. Plant them by the side of the road, hit the remote trigger device as the convoy comes by.
It takes Chon three days to build them.
Happy hours on the old dining room table.
'You're not going to blow us up, are you?' Ben asks.
'We should be okay,' Chon says. 'Unless the BC has a drone overhead or something. Then we're fucked. But I wouldn't use the TV remote for a while.'
Just to be on the safe side.

Ben asks, 'What should I do if I hear you mutter, "Fuck"?'

'At this range? Nothing.'

A lot of existential questions will be answered just after the 'Fuck.'

As in life itself.

222

The caravan comes up the twisted road.

Like a coiled snake, the Cajon Pass. Way the fuck out there in the empty desert, miles away from anything that could pass for civilization.

Moonscape on either side of the road.

God threw a temper tantrum and tossed boulders around like marbles on the steep slopes.

Turning red in the dawn light.

The reflection makes it tough on Chon, high up on the opposite slope, sighting the Barrett.

He hopes Ben is cold enough to throw the switches.

223

Lead car, cash car, follow car.

Escalade, Taurus, Suburban.

The Escalade is far out in front, maybe fifty yards, the Suburban is tight on the Taurus.

Ben crouches in the rocks not far from the road.

Remote controls for toy airplanes in his hand.

Two toggle switches.

They've been out there all night, planting the

IEDs. Studied this road on Google Earth, looked for the right narrow hairpin curve, close to rocks that will contain and channel the blast.

Non-symmetrical conflict.

It won't be self-defense this time, it will be out-and-out murder.

The men in the caravan must be fairly relaxed. They came up from the flat desert and could see any car for miles, and saw nothing.

There's nothing out here.

Ben waits.

Hand trembles.

With adrenaline, or doubt?

224

The caravan comes into the narrow switchback.
Chon sights in. In his mind's eye, though, he sees—
 —Taliban

    moving like scorpions across a
    similar landscape
      his own caravan blown to
      shit
        blood streaming from
        buddies

 Now I'm one of *them*
He sights in again. No time for
  Lack of PTSD
He only hopes that
Gentle Ben

Increase-the-Peace Ben
             is one of them, too, now.
Now, Ben.
Find your inner Taliban.

225

Ben peeks above the sheltering boulder and sees the three vehicles come into the pass.

The cars themselves are nothing – assembly-line products of plastic and steel, little Bunsen burners of global warming. Dinosaur carbon prints on the sere landscape. They are *things,* and Ben has no compunctions about things ('we are spirits in the material world'). Tries to tell himself that they are *only* things but he knows. the truth – there are people inside the things.

Beings with families, friends, loved ones, hopes, fears.

Capable, unlike the vessels that carry them, of pain and suffering.

Which he is about to inflict.

Index finger and thumb poised on the switch.

A simple muscle fiber twitch but

There is no Undo button.

No Control Alt Delete

Ben thinks about suicide bombers

Murder is the suicide of the soul.

He takes his hand off.

Now, Ben, Chon thinks. Now or never.

Now or not at all.

Two more seconds and the moment will have passed.

Ben flips the switch.

A blast of flame and the lead car hops sideways.

Shredded.

The cash car speeds up to pull around it but

Chon squeezes the trigger of the Barrett Model 90 and

The driver's face disappears, red (incarnadine) with the daybreak, then

Its passenger leans in to take the wheel as

Chon slides the bolt back, reloads, sights, and shoots a big ragged hole into the would-be hero's chest and then the car rolls into the rocks, stops, and bursts into flame.

Men, rifles in their hands, start to get out of the follow car but

Ben flips the second switch and fragments of the Escalade become shrapnel, tearing, ripping, killing, and what it doesn't do

Chon does.

The survivors of the blast – stunned, shocked, and bleeding – look up and around as if to ask the question where does death come from

it comes from
Chon, sliding the bolt, pulling the trigger, and
in seconds
It is quiet except for
The crackling of flames and the
Groans of the wounded.

228

Chon drops the rifle, it
Clatters on the rocks and he
Scampers down the slope, gets into the work
car, pulled off on the side, covered in brush, and
he races it down to where
Ben
      his face lit by flame
      stands among the dead and dying.
'Get the money,' Chon says. He reaches under
the dead driver's legs and releases the trunk.
It opens with a dull pop.
Canvas bags full of cash.
They heft them and carry them to their own car
and come back for more and Ben hears the shot
and sees Chon whirl and fall and Ben
Head on a swivel, turns and shoots the shooter,
dying anyway.
Ben pulls Chon up from the dust, helps him to
the work car, sits him in the passenger seat. Starts
to get behind the wheel but Chon says, 'Get the
rest of the cash. And Ben, you know what you
have to do.'

Ben grabs the two remaining satchels and tosses them into the car.

Then he walks back.

He does know

What he has to do.

Wounded survivors could identify them

And kill O.

He finds three men still alive.

Fetal, curled in pain.

He shoots each of them in the back of the head.

229

Fuck that.

Chon's response to Ben's 'We have to get you to a hospital.'

Chon rips off a piece of his shirt, presses it to his shoulder, down on the wound, and keeps pressing.

'Where's the nearest hospital?' Ben asks.

'You go to a hospital with a gunshot wound,' Chon says calmly, 'the first thing they do is call the cops. Drive to Ocotillo Wells.'

'Are you out of your fucking mind?' Ben answers, his hands trembling on the wheel. There's no hospital in Ocotillo Wells. It's a little desert shit-hole that services the four-wheeler, off-road types.

'Ocotillo Wells,' Chon answers.

'Okay.'

'You're doing great.'

274

'Just don't die,' Ben says. 'Stay with me. Isn't that what you're supposed to say?'

Chon laughs.

Chon is so cool.

Been There Before.

In Stanland. Convoy ambushed. Narrow mountain road. Shit flying, people hurt, you either stay cool or your people die, you die. You don't do that, you stay cool, you get—

Everybody Out.

Speaking of which—

230

Ben pulls alongside the Airstream trailer off a dirt road in the Middle of Nowhere.

Tumbleweeds tossing around like they blew off a movie set. Jury-rigged power line jacked from a phone pole to the trailer. An old pickup and a Dodge GT parked under a homemade *remada* built of willow poles.

'Pull it up close,' Chon instructs. 'Go knock on the door, tell Doc you got me with you and that I took one.'

Ben gets out.

Legs feel like old rubber, loose and shaky.

He goes up the wooden steps to the trailer door and knocks. Hears, 'Oh-three-thirty, this better be fucking good.'

Door opens, a guy about their age stares at him. Boxer shorts and nothing else on, disheveled, eyes red, he looks at Ben and says, 'If you're some fucking Jehovah's Witness or something I'm going to kick your ass.'

'It's Chon. He's shot.'

'Get him in here.'

231

Ken 'Doc' Lorenzen, former medic on Chon's SEAL team, is one cool cat.

You don't believe it, you should have seen him at that ambush scene – dry ice in triple-digit heat – moving from one wounded man to the next with deliberate haste – as if bullets weren't coming in at him, as if he weren't a target. If it hadn't been so serious it would have been comical, Doc out there with his weird body shape – short legs, short trunk, long arms – distributing life-saving medical assistance. What Doc did that day should have earned him the MOH but Doc didn't care.

Doc did his job.

He got Everyone Out.

Now he lives in this trailer off his pension and disability, pounds beer, eats Hormel chili and Dinty Moore beef stew, watches baseball on his little TV and looks at porn except when he can pull a four-wheeler chick off her dune buggy, one who doesn't mind a trailer.

It's a decent life.

He sweeps crushed beer cans, newspapers, porn

mags, and a bag of Cheetos off the 'kitchen' table. Chon hops up and then lies down.

'Is that sterile?' Ben asks.

'Don't tell me how to do my job. Go boil some water or something.'

'You need water boiled?'

'No, but if it will keep your piehole shut . . .'

He finds his kit under a crumpled wet-suit, scissors Chon's shirt off, and probes the shoulder. 'You got a movie wound, brother. Fleshy part of the shoulder. Must have nicked the Kevlar and bounced up.'

'Is it still in there?'

'Oh yeah.'

'Can you get it out?'

'Oh yeah.'

You kidding me? Simple surgery in a (sort of) clean, air-conditioned trailer with no IEDs going off and nobody shooting at him?

Gimme putt.

Tap it in with your foot if you want.

He takes out a wound pad and creates a sterile field. Pours a glass of iso and dips his instruments into it.

Ben sees the scalpel.

'You going to give him some whiskey or something?' he asks.

'Seriously, who are you?' Doc answers. He takes out a vial of morphine. 'By the way, what mischief have you children been up to that my boy here isn't at Scripps?'

277

Chon answers, 'You got any beer left?'
'I don't remember.'
'Morphine and beer?' Ben asks.
'Is not just for breakfast anymore,' Doc replies.
He fills the syringe and finds a nice vein.

232

Ben goes out and counts the money.
$3.5 million. O numbers.
Mission accomplished.

233

Even in Southern California, even in the middle of the desert, you don't leave six dead Mexicans among the smoldering ruins of three cars without attracting *some* attention.

SoCal takes its cars very seriously.

Mexicans die in the desert all the time.

It's not a daily event, but it's not headline news, either. Mostly these are *mujados* trying to cross the border in the hot wild region between San Diego and El Centro and either they get lost on their own or the coyotes dump them out there and they die of sunstroke or thirst. It's gotten to the point that the Border Patrol leaves caches of water marked with red flags on high poles because the BP agents don't want the endless game of hide-and-seek to be actually lethal.

Mexican drug dealers?

That's another story, literally.

You expect this sort of shit South of the Border – it is a daily event, a tedious *tsk-tsk* head-line-cum-photos of dead and or decapitated bodies, shot-up, bombed-out vehicles with a confusing enchilada plate of Spanish names and words like 'cartel' and 'war on drugs' and usually a comment from a DEA official.

You expect it down there, that's what you expect from those people.

And you expect the occasional gang echo in the barrios of San Diego, Los Angeles, and even certain parts of Orange County. (Certain parts – that is, Santa Ana or Anaheim – you leave it out of Irvine and Newport Beach, *amigos*. Just clean the pools and go home.)

But a full-out Mexican-style firefight – freaking bombs and burned-out cars – on *this* side of the border?

That's too much, Jack.

That is outrageous.

That's downright scary is what that is.

This has the radio talk-show hosts so titillated they're shifting their fat ass cheeks in their chairs because it looks like

La Reconquista

The Mexican Invasion

What Everyone Has Been Warning About All These Years but the Federal Government Just Won't Listen. (Bush needed the Mexican vote and Obama . . . well, Obama's an illegal immigrant, too, isn't he? An undocumented worker in the White House. Too bad there's no fucking deserts in Hawaii.)

Suffice it to say

There's heat on this one.

It even gets Dennis off his butt. His supervisor tells him to get his ass out to East County and find out just what the hell is going on out there because

It is what it looks like.

A *tombe,* in the jargon of the trade.

Dennis is up on developments.

He knows about the BC Civil War.

Not, by the way, the worst thing in the world, if you can get over your squeamishness; Dennis is firmly of the opinion, for instance, that the U.S. was better off when Iran and Iraq were bleeding each other to death, but the bodies are supposed to be stacked up South of the Border or in Designated Gang Areas, not on a public highway.

Californians take their highways very seriously. It's where they drive their freaking cars.

Dennis knows of Lado's new rules and regs, knows that he's looking at a lead car-cash car-follow car parade that didn't quite make it to the finish line.

Another agent out there who recently completed an informational tour of Afghanistan recognizes the signs of IED explosions – two of them – which seems to confirm the rumor that the cartels have taken to hiring recently discharged American servicemen.

Dennis fervently hopes the cartels haven't also taken to hiring recently discharged Taliban, because that would cause a clusterfuck of monumental proportions with the professional paranoids at Homeland Security.

(Condition *Scarlet*!!!!)

The other interesting little bit of forensic joy is the presence of horrible gaping wounds apparently caused by .50-caliber bullets and the local CHP troopers' somewhat overenthused opinion that they were fired by some apparent superweapon called a Barrett 90, hard to acquire and reputedly harder to handle, so we're looking at a professional job here.

Really? Dennis thinks as he looks at a scene straight out of the evening news. (Please, merciful God in heaven, don't let the networks pick this up.) No shit? Three cars full of *narcotraficantes* taken out with IEDs and a superrifle and you don't think it was done by a bunch of local high school kids with nothing else to do so we need to build them a freaking community center with a Ping-Pong table and a skateboard tube?!

Dennis drives back to the relative civilization of urban San Diego with the stomach-churning thought that things are

Out Of Control.

Doc has radio streaming on his laptop.

Satellite reception.

He uses it to listen to Jim Rome.

Now he gets news of a Stanland-style shootout not so far from here and Doc is no idiot. He looks at Chon.

Chon hasn't changed much since back in the day.

When Chon announced that AQ stood for

Asses Qicked.

And ass-kicked a whole unit of them barricaded inside a compound in Doha. It took him all day but Chon was patient, methodical, in no hurry at all. Came back, scoffed three MREs, and went horizontal. Slept like a sated baby. So a six-pack of narcos? Not a problem, piece o' cake.

Chon and Ben watch Doc listen to the news report, add two plus two, and come up with Chon.

Doc says, 'We'd better get rid of your car. You can take my Dodge.'

'Thank you, man.'

'*Nada.*'

They drive the work car up a ravine, Doc following in his pickup. He takes cans of gas out of the truck bed and douses the work car. Lights a book of matches and tosses it through the open passenger window.

No time for hot dogs or s'mores, though.

Instead, Doc hooks Chon up with some

ampoules of morphine and a few syringes and wishes him

Godspeed.

235

Driving back to the OC, Chon is all, like, what did you expect?

He's blasé.

(Yeah, the morphine helps.)

Six dead Mexicans is a light day in, uhhh, Mexico, and the fact that they're lying on this side of the border is less than *nada* to him.

Borders are a state of mind, and he's accustomed to a certain mental flexibility when it comes to national borders, like the alleged line between Afghanistan and Pakistan. They were both just Stans in his mind, and if the Taliban didn't care, he sure as hell didn't. Then there was that border between Syria and Iraq, which was a little nebulous (*good* word, nebulous) for a while until a few people in Syria went for the long walk.

Ben is too aware that borders are a state of mind.

There are mental borders and there are moral borders and you cross the first you can maybe make the round trip but if you cross the second you're not ever coming back. Your return ticket is canceled.

Go Ask Alex.

'Don't do it,' Chon says.

'Don't do what?'

'Don't waste your energy feeling guilty about these guys,' Chon says, 'or Alex or any of them.'

May I remind you that these are the guys who—

—beheaded people
—tortured kids
and
—kidnapped O.

'They had it coming?' Ben asks.

'Yeah.'

Keep it simple.

'Collective punishment.'

'You don't need to put labels to everything, B,' Chon says.

The world isn't a moral supermarket. Clean-up on aisle three.

236

Chon has read a lot of history.

The Romans used to send their legions out to the fringes of the empire to kill barbarians. That's what they did for hundreds of years, but then they stopped doing it. Because they were too distracted, too busy fucking, drinking, gorging themselves. So busy squabbling over power they forgot who they were, forgot their culture, forgot to defend it.

The barbarians came in.

And it was over.

'So let's pay them off,' he says to Ben now, 'get O back, and get the fuck out of here.'

It's over.

237

Elena can't hear a thing, only the loud incessant throb in her ears and she doesn't know what happened at first, she only realizes it was a bomb when she looks out the car window and sees the man, one of *her* men, grip his shredded arm, and then the car surges forward, speeding through the streets of Tijuana's Rio Colonia, running through traffic lights and then through the gate which is open but closes right behind her and then one of the *sicarios* opens the car door, pulls her out, and trots her into the house and it's several minutes later, quite a few actually, when she realizes that they tried to kill her.

'The children?!' she shouts as she gets into the house.

Her new head of security, Beltran, answers, 'They're fine. We checked it out. We have them.'

Thank God, thank God, thank God, Elena thinks. She asks, 'Magda?'

'We're on her. She's fine.'

She's at Starbucks near campus, sitting at her laptop, apparently writing a paper. Lado has two men across the street.

'I want to talk with her.'

'She doesn't know anything about—'

'Get her on her cell.'

A few moments later she hears Magda's slightly irritated voice. 'Hello, Mama.'

'Hello, darling. I just wanted to hear your voice.'

Magda lets a small silence intrude to let her mother know that she's interrupting something substantial for sentimental maternal nonsense and then says, 'Well, this is my voice, Mama.'

'Are you well?'

'I'm busy.'

Meaning she's well.

'I'll let you go, then,' Elena says, a small quiver of relief in her voice.

'I'll call you this weekend.'

'I'll look forward to that.' Elena takes a real breath.

'I'll be down in a few minutes,' she tells her men.

It's silly, but what she wants is a bath and she rings Carmelita to get it ready but the men won't let Carmelita or anyone else up to the second floor, so, annoyed, she draws it herself.

The hot water feels good on her skin, she feels the muscles in her lower back loosen, hadn't realized that they were so tight. She sits up to open the hot water tap again and then realizes that she can now hear the water running and couldn't before and she lets herself lie in the tub for ten more minutes before she gets out, gets dressed, and takes charge again.

Queen Elena.

This is my life now.

She puts on a severe black sweater over jeans and goes downstairs.

The men are waiting in the dining room.

'We think it was El Azul,' Salazar says. A colonel of the state police, he is unimaginative but reliable as long as the money holds out.

'Of course it was him,' Elena snaps. 'The question is how did his men get so close?'

'It was an IED,' says Beltran, twice removed from the much-missed Lado. The man who held the job in between was El Azul.

'Explain?'

'Improvised explosive device,' Beltran says. 'Basically a bomb planted near your route, detonated by remote control.'

Elena shakes her head. 'How many killed?'

'Five. Three of ours, two civilians.'

Elena says, 'Find the families, pay the funeral expenses.'

'I feel strongly,' Beltran says, 'that you should go to the *finca* for a while, where we can look after you.'

'You're supposed to be looking after me *here*,' Elena says. She stares at him until his eyes drop and he looks at the table. She sighs and says, 'Very well, I will go to the *finca*.'

The door opens and Hernan bursts in.

'Mother, I just heard. Thank God.'

He kisses her cheek, turns to Beltran, and yells, 'Why aren't you doing your job?! I swear, if my mother had been hurt . . .'

287

Hernan doesn't finish the threat. Instead he says, 'We have to respond to this. We can't let them think they can act with impunity. Find who did this and—'

'We know who they are,' Beltran says.

Elena looks at him, surprised.

'Azul is recruiting soldiers in the States,' Beltran explains. 'Literally soldiers – Mexicans fresh out of the U.S. Army. They know how to do these IEDs. They learned it in Iraq.'

'Get them,' Hernan says.

'They're probably across the border already.'

'Give it to Lado,' Elena says.

238

O and Esteban like to smoke up, eat pizza, and watch *The Biggest Loser*.

Bolting fat greasy carbs while stone-watching a show about people trying to lose weight is perverse enough to satisfy O's boredom and, as has been mentioned, the girl likes to grub.

Esteban just likes smoking up, watching television, and being with O.

The pizza, too. Tonight's is an extra-large pepperoni with hamburger, green pepper, and extra cheese. Esteban doesn't like the green pepper but he does like to keep O happy.

Anyway, O is fascinated that she's fascinated with the idea of watching an activity that you can't actually *see*. It's like, tele*vision*, right, but you can't see fat burning inside any of these obese bodies. But you can watch them sweat and groan and cry, and in addition to the pure pleasure of troughing out while they're starving, O has developed an affection for some of them.

It's, like, they're trying to *do* something.

Change their lives for the better.

It's admirable.

Unlike yourself, she says to herself one night.

'Let's face it,' she says to Esteban, 'I'm pretty much a useless twat.'

Esteban knows 'useless' – *fregado* – he doesn't know 'twat.'

'When I get out of here,' O says, '*if* I get out of here—'

'You will.'

'I'm going to do something with my life.'

'What?'

Well, that's the prob, *ese*, Este.

I have no fucking idea.

239

Lado crawls into bed.

To give the wife a little.

What she needs, a good stiff dick.

He nudges his between the warm cheeks of her ass and rubs it up and down, seeking an invitation.

Delores gets up and out of bed. 'Give it to your *putana*. I don't want it.'

Lado's in no mood. He has a lot on his mind. The war, the *tombe*, now the attempt on Elena and increased security on her brat of a daughter, who doesn't think she needs security. And now Delores forgets her place. 'Get your butt back here.'

'No thank you.'

'I said get your fucking ass back in this bed.'

'Make me.'

Okay, that's a mistake.

He's out of the sheets in a flash. She's forgotten how quick he is, how strong he is – the first slap sends her reeling against the wall, her ears ringing as he grabs her, throws her on the bed, lands on top of her, pins both wrists above her head with his one big hand.

He pushes her thighs apart with his knee.

'This the way you want it, bitch?'

'I *don't* want it.'

Maybe not, but she gets it.

He takes his time, too.

Afterward, coming out of the bathroom, she says, 'I want a divorce.'

He laughs. 'You want *what*?'

'A divorce.'

'What you're going to get is a beating,' Lado says, 'you don't shut your mouth now.'

Delores backs into the doorway. 'I already talked to a lawyer. He said I'd get half the house, the money, custody of the kids . . .'

Lado nods.

He could beat the fucking shit out of her but he has something worse for her than a beating. He smiles and says, 'Delores, if you go through with this, I will take the kids to Mexico and you will never, ever see them again. You know that's the truth, you know I'll do it, so stop acting foolish and come back to bed.'

She stands in the doorway for a few seconds.

She knows him.

Who he is.

What he does.

She gets back in bed.

240

Elena packs a few things.

She only needs a few things because she has complete sets of everything she needs at all her residences. Each house, she thinks, sits full and ready, waiting only for my presence to complete its emptiness.

There's a knock on the door and she knows from its tentativeness that it's Hernan. She lets him in and he asks, 'Are you ready to go to the *finca*?'

'Yes, all ready.'

They go downstairs, then out into the courtyard and into the car that has been specially fitted with armor siding. Beltran, anxious, hovers like a mother hen, sees them into the car, and gets into a heavily armed Suburban in front of them.

They drive several blocks, then Elena orders the driver to take a left.

'The *finca* is the other way, Mother.'

She says, 'We're not going to the *finca*.'

He looks confused.

Of course he does, the poor darling, so she continues. 'The plan was for us to go to the *finca*, where Beltran would have had us assassinated. He set the bomb – if it didn't kill me, it would have driven me to seek safety at the ranch under his protection.'

Her laugh is bitter.

'How did you know?'

How didn't *you* know, Elena thinks, is more the question. And the problem. She cannot leave him in Mexico, he wouldn't survive five minutes. She will have to take him with, and arrange for his *bruja* wife to follow after.

Before she can answer, Beltran's Suburban does a U-turn to follow her, but two other cars appear from a side alley and block the way. Elena looks out the back window as men with AK-47s jump out of the two cars and open up on the Suburban.

Beltran comes out of the passenger side firing, but they riddle him with bullets and he melts into the pavement.

'You can go now,' Elena says to the driver.

The car moves ahead.

'Why didn't you tell me?' Hernan asks.

'Could you have pulled it off?' she asks. 'Disguised your feelings, smiled, and shook his hand?'

'No.'

'Well, then.' She pats his hand, sighs, and says, 'I'm tired of war, tired of the killing, the worry. I have been for some time. So I've prepared a move. We're going to the United States. Lado has prepared the ground for us. Your sisters are there already.'

Azul wants Baja? she ponders.

Fine, he can have it.

Good luck to him.

'To America?' Hernan asks. 'What about the police? The DEA?'

She smiles.

Oh, my darling boy.

241

Dear Mom-O,

London is XQZT. And swings like a pendulum do. Did you know that Big Ben is the clock and not the tower? I didn't. And the Tower of London is really interesting. A lot of people got their heads cut off there. Like, yech, right? Good thing they don't do that anymore, except I guess they do in some Arab countries like Arabia. Anyway, it's really cool here. Okay, it's off to Trafalgar Square and later to the West End to see a play. I might even give Shakespere a try! Who'd a thunk, huh?

Miss U

143,
O (for short)

When O and Esteban aren't watching TV on Hulu, they're on Google and Wikipedia looking up stuff on the cities that O is visiting on the European travels that she's e-mailing Paqu about.

'She's, like, a detail freak,' O explains to Esteban, 'so I have to get the little things right.'

The crazy thing is that Paqu never writes her back.

Too busy with Jesus, O guesses.

242

Spin looks gloriously ridiculous this morning in a skintight Ferrari cycling suit with a Cinzano cap.

The thing you gotta love about Spin is that he doesn't even blink when Ben shows up with twenty mil in assets and cash and says it needs to go on the superfast cycle but come *back* as all cash, albeit squeaky clean.

An IRS sort of thing – Ben might have to have a nice explanation as to how he got the money, something other than he took it from the same people he's about to give it to. He doesn't say this exactly to Spin, but he doesn't need to.

Spin sits down at his laptop and

—sells Ben's house to one of Ben's own companies, then to a resident of Vanuatu who doesn't exist, then—

—off-loads a bunch of Ben's stocks and bonds to a holding company Ben owns, then—

—creates a small ranch in Argentina, puts cattle on it, sells the cattle, and—

'Your cash is immaculate.'

Spin gets back on his bike.

Ben goes to see Jaime.

243

'Where did you get it?'

Jaime asks, looking at the briefcases full of cash.

'What difference does it make?' Ben asks, figuring a lack of resistance might arouse suspicion.

'We have some money missing.'

'Gee, that's too bad.'

Ben explains that some of the cash came from the short money they've been paying him for his 420, the rest came from selling about everything he owns, thank you very much for that, BTW.

'We'll need documentation.'

Ben gives him the computer-code keys to the kingdom and tells him to knock himself out.

'I'm transparent,' he says.

Just hurry it up.

Jaime hurries it up.

It all checks out.

'Why didn't you just do this before?' Jaime asks.

'You tried selling a house these days?' Ben answers. 'As it is, I took a thumping on it. Make the call, Jaime.'

Jaime makes the call.

Elena personally okays it.

She's glad, truly glad, that she can let the girl go.

244

Esteban comes into O's room looking almost sad.

'They're going to let you go,' he says.

WDYS?

'Your friends paid the money,' Esteban says. 'We're going to take you back.'

O starts to cry.

Esteban's a little choked up, too.

Summoning up his courage, he asks her to be his Facebook friend.

245

They text the instructions:

Be ready at 2PM. We'll text you the location.

'You trust these motherfuckers?' Chon asks.

Jump – I'll catch you.

'No, but do we have a choice?'

No.

Dear Maternal Unit,

I'm clicking my ruby slippers.

:Europe is like, way cool and all that, but 'there's no place like home,' right? Plus, I'm about out of money, but I guess you guessed that already.

Now Momzoid, when I say I'm coming home, I don't mean home *home. Well, for a little bit, maybe, but then I'm going to move out. About time, huh-duh? The thing of it is, I think I need to create a* life, *you know. (Sans coach, that is.) I'm not even sure yet what that really means, but it has to mean something. I might even go overseas (again) to do some humanatarian work. You know, like aid stuff. You remember my friend Ben? I might go with him and another friend, Chon, to do some useful type stuff in Indoneesia. Dig wells or something like that. CanU picture that? Your useless little girl with a shovel in her hands?*

Luv u,
O

Gun shop Barney is an inveterate listener to right-wing talk-show radio.

Anyway, Barney hears all about the massacre on the highway and gleans the additional news, welcome other than the fact that he has six less Mexicans to worry about. What he hears is the leaked info about the .50 rounds found in and around the said dead Cans and the speculation that the first shots were fired from a distance—

—well no fucking shit, you don't use no Barrett Model 90 for close work—

—and he sees a chance to do himself some good.

See, Barney lives on the border.

Yeah, okay, everyone in this fucking life does, but Barney lives on the *border* and what that really means these days is that he lives as much in Mexico as he does in the USofA.

He don't like it, he ain't happy about it, but the facts is the facts.

Don't matter what the Border Patrol says, what the Minutemen say, what any dickhead in DC says, this country is run as much or more by the Baja Cartel.

Just something Barney had to work with.

Which he does pretty well, seeing as how they're his best customer.

He don't let that out, because his *second*-best customers are the right-wingers, who, like Barney, *hate* Mexicans, but Barney's got stacks and stacks of medical bills, the Bureau of Alcohol, Tobacco, Firearms and Explosives is all *over* his ass – we're talking the possibility of him spending his golden years dodging the niggers and the shit in a federal penitentiary – so now he has a choice to make.

Which government does he call?

Which one can he trust?

Which will do him the most good?

He turns down the radio so he can talk on the phone.

Lado is very pleased to hear from him and believes, yes, they *can* do a little 'horse tradin'.'

(Gringo cracker *pendejo.*)

Then Lado hears which pony ole Barney has to trade and

—he's not happy.

248

Lado isn't happy, but Elena is furious.

Out of her skull angry.

Because she feels like a fool.

She let these Americans dupe her and now she wonders if she let her fondness for (or fascination with?) the girl get in the way of her better judgment.

Settling into the new American house—

Well, *compound,* really, a new fortress set in the remote desert, with more yards of barbed wire, alarms, sound and motion sensors, armed men patrolling in four-wheel-drive vehicles and ATVs, all on high alert since the last assassination attempts—

—is sadly easy. Another set of clothes, sets of linens, towels, toiletries, kitchen appliances that have never been used to fix a meal, all as sterile as her present life. Lado's wife, the perfect hostess, a lady-in-waiting, has come personally to see that everything is in order. Even the surrounding desert seems too clean – scrubbed by wind and bleached by the sun, an exterior to match her sparse interior landscape.

Thirst.

She thinks about her new life as a refugee.

A billionaire *mujado,* a wetback with greenbacks.

Lado has prepared this (sere) ground against this day, when the cartel would have to leave Mexico and take up a new existence in this new and savage land. Everything is in place – the safe houses, stash houses, the markets, and the men. The DEA generously bribed, her presence here duly un-noted.

She had hoped to leave the bloodletting behind, and now this.

A war that came with her.

A betrayal of her trust.

And now the necessity to commit yet another atrocity.

She gets on the phone to Lado.

'Bring Magda here.'

'She won't want to come.'

'Did I ask you what she wants?' Elena snaps.

The silence of acquiescence. She's used to that in men – passivity is their small rebellion. It seems to keep their precious *cojones* in place.

Then Lado asks, cruelly, 'What about the girl? The other one.'

'We have no choice but to follow through.'

'I agree.'

Did I ask if you agreed? Elena thinks, but keeps the thought to herself. What she's asking him to do is enough without adding her bitchiness to it. She knows what's behind it, too – she doesn't want to kill this girl.

Elena sits down at the computer and turns on the monitor.

The girl is in her room – at a ranch just a few miles away – lying on her back, doing her nails.

In preparation, Elena thinks, for going home.

You do not want to kill this girl because she reminds you of your own wild child, of yourself during your brief flash of freedom in what now seems another lifetime.

Well, if you do not wish to kill her, don't.

It is your choice, you don't have to answer to anyone.

Elena recognizes this for what it is – a moment of rebellion against the present state of her life, against what she's become.

A forlorn hope.

If you do not kill this girl – if you do not do exactly what you promised to do – then you put your own children at risk. Because the savages will see you as weak, and they will come for you and yours.

Lado has waited patiently.

She says, 'Do it. And I want them to see it.'

I am the Red Queen.

Off with her head.

'Do you want to be there?' Lado asks.

'No,' Elena says.

But she'll make herself watch it on the screen. If you can order it, she demands of herself, you can watch it.

'I want it done before Magda gets here,' she adds.

'It will take me a little time to get there,' Lado says.

'As soon as possible, please,' she says. She has another thought. 'Get in touch with these bastards. Let them know.'

Let them suffer.

249

Ben and Chon wait by the computer.

The instructions come at two o'clock.

You can watch her die at 6.
We know you did it.
You're next.

They have four hours.

To do what?

They know she's at one of three places in the desert, but what are they going to do? Pick one and hope they get lucky? And even if it is the right place—

'We'd never make it in,' Chon says. 'And they'd kill her when the shooting started.'

'What are we going to do?' Ben asks. 'Sit and watch?'

'No,' Chon says.

We're not going to do that.

251

CI 1459 has given Dennis a lot of good shit over the years.

Helped him take down two of the Lauter brothers and put them in jail. Put a few straws in the broom with which Dennis tried to sweep back the ocean of drugs coming from the Baja Cartel.

In turn Dennis rewarded him with a

Green Card

Sanctuary

A New Identity.

Now Lado calls to tell him something that he already knows – Elena Sanchez Lauter is on her way to a 'safe house' in the desert.

He gives Dennis the exact location.

Did the dumb cunt think that he was preparing

the ground for her? The years of work, of killing, for her and not himself? Yes, Your Majesty. *Si*, Elena La Reina?

So the DEA will arrest Elena, and no one can blame Lado. And no one will want the weak-kneed son to take her place so there will be nowhere to turn but him. And he will make El Azul a peace offer – a fifty-fifty split of the American *plaza*.

Azul will not refuse.

It's a home run.

252

Dennis gets in the car.

'They have the girl,' Ben says.

'Who?'

'The girl you met with us,' Chon says. 'They're going to kill her.'

Ben says, 'Elena Sanchez Lauter has a daughter, Magdalena. She's a student at Irvine.'

'Jesus, Ben.'

'Where is she?'

'Are you out of your mind?' Dennis asks.

'Yes,' Ben says. 'Tell us where to find her.'

Dennis looks down at his gut. When he looks up his eyes are wet. 'I'm into them, Ben. Big-time. Mid-six figures.'

'Fuck, Dennis.'

'Fuck, indeed, Ben.'

'Where's the daughter?'

'Jesus, Ben, they'll kill my family.'

'I'll give you money,' Ben says. 'Run with your family, tonight. But you're going to tell me.'

Dennis thinks about this for a second, then gets out of the car. The northbound Metrolink is coming up from Oceanside. The train where you can see dolphins and whales from the seaside windows.

He walks over to the track. Ben jumps out of the car. Too late.

Dennis steps onto the rails.

253

'She has to live somewhere,' Chon says. She does.

They go through Steve's real estate list again.

An apartment in Irvine.

MapQuest.

Three blocks from campus.

254

Truism.

Cliché.

You become what you hate.

Ben says, 'You know what we have to do.'

Chon knows.

255

Lado's man gets out of the car in the parking lot of Magda's apartment building.

Pop-pop.

Chon puts two silenced rounds in the back of his head and then puts him back in the car.

The drug war comes to Irvine.

256

Magda fixes herself a cup of green tea.

She wants a little boost but she's coffee'd out and, anyway, the tea is healthier. Antioxidants and all that.

The doorbell rings.

She doesn't know who it could be and she's a little annoyed because what she wants right now is to put her feet up, drink her tea, and read a hundred pages of Insoll for her arch and religion course.

Probably Leslie, the lazy slut, coming over to borrow her notes. If the *puta* could get up in the morning to get to class—

'Leslie . . . God . . .'

Magda opens the door and the guy is on her like that, one hand over her mouth, the other behind her neck pushing her back down and onto the sofa. She hears the door shut and sees a second guy come in and he puts a gun to the side of her head.

She shakes her head, like, take anything you want, *do* anything you want. Thank God the guy puts the gun back in his belt, but then he has a syringe and he grabs her arm, rolls up the sleeve of her black silk blouse, and jabs the needle in her vein.

Then she's out.

257

Lado pulls up outside the house and gets out.

Esteban opens the door.

The *mierdita* looks like he's been crying.

Lado moves past him into the room where they keep the little blonde *puta*. She sees his face and knows. Knows and starts to run but he cuffs her across the face, grabs her by the wrist, and pulls her into the other room. Shoves her little ass down into the chair, takes off his belt, and straps her hands behind it.

She's kicking her feet and screaming.

Lado yells, 'Help me, *pendejo*. Hold her fucking legs.'

Esteban keeps crying but he does what he's told. He grabs her by the feet and holds on while Lado gets the duct tape and forces it onto her mouth. Then he squats down and wraps a length around her ankles and the chair legs.

'Don't worry, *chucha*,' he says. 'Your legs will be wide open later. You can count on that.'

He goes to straighten up and Esteban has a gun out, pointed at him.

258

When Magda comes to, still groggy, they have her strapped up with duct tape.

She's in some kind of cheap motel room.

A laptop computer is set on the coffee table in front of her, the little camera eye red and blinking, and she thinks this is some kind of twisted Internet porno rape and if it is she wants them to just get it over with and not kill her.

But neither of the men takes his clothes off or even unzips his jeans.

One starts typing on the keyboard, the other

Pulls the gun out again and jacks a round into the chamber

259

'What are you going to do with that?' Lado asks.

Esteban, the little ball of shit, his hands are shaking. Reminds Lado of the old car they had out back as a kid. When you started the engine the whole car would quiver and rattle and that's what Esteban's hands look like now.

'Let her go,' Esteban says

and then Lado knows he's in no danger because this kid didn't listen to him when he told him you pull a gun you pull the trigger you don't threaten or talk you

pull the trigger

260

'Log on,' Ben says.

Log the fuck on, Lado.

261

The bullet misses.

Not by much, but life, like baseball, is a game of inches.

Lado steps in, knocks the pistol from the boy's hand, grabs him by the head, and twists.

Esteban's neck snaps.

Like kindling.

Lado turns on the camera and aims it at the girl. Then he turns on the computer and types in the address.

Then he picks up the chain saw.

262

Skype.
Ben and Chon see
A rerun
O strapped to the chair
Lado standing with the chain saw.

O's eyes wide with terror. Fresh dialogue, though.

'Maybe I fuck her before I kill her,' Lado says. He turns toward O. 'You like that, little whore? One last dick?'

263

Elena forces herself to sit down at the computer.
She logs on and sees

Magda
With a gun to her head.
Fuck you.

Love makes you strong.
Love makes you weak.
Elena asks, 'What do you want?'

                                        CUT TO:

INT. SPLIT SCREEN – MOTEL ROOM/ELENA'S
COMPOUND/DESERT SAFE HOUSE

BEN
You know what we want.

ELENA
Don't do this. I'm begging you.

BEN
We want the girl back. Unharmed.

ELENA
Do what they say, Lado.

LADO

Of course. *(To BEN)* Take it easy.

BEN

We will kill her. We'll do it.

ELENA

I believe you. We can work this out. We'll set a time and place for the exchange. Please don't do anything rash.

267

Lado sets the time and place.

268

Because why the fuck not? Lado thinks.
Why the fuck not.
Lado is a cake-and-eat-it-too kind of guy.
So maybe he doesn't cut the *puta's* head off. No big loss. He will kill her, only a little later, and he'll kill them, too.
As for Elena's stuck-up bitch of a daughter
Who gives a fuck?

269

'You know what's going to happen,' Chon says.
Ben knows.
They'll go to exchange their hostages—

—*fuck* Ben hates that word, *hates* that he has a hostage – Elena will show up with an army.
Their chances of getting out alive are
How many ways are there to say zero?
    Nothing.
    Empty
    No
        hope, no
        faith, no
        values, no
        future, no
        past.
Nothingness.

270

The e-mail arrived after they took O from the compound, so she didn't read:

My darling girl,

I am so sorry that I've been out of touch. It is from no lack of love for you, my darling darling, but for the love of the Lord. I have been on a retreat to contemplate the state of my soul, and we were allowed no communications with the outside world.

This world is corrupt, Ophelia. The flesh is weak.

Only the soul survives.

Ophelia, I have met a man!

I know you have heard this before – too many times – but this time it's the real thing. John knows and loves the Lord, too, and now that we are back from the retreat we intend to marry and start a jewelry business – bracelets and necklaces that will proclaim the wearer's faith. With my sense of style and John's business acumen – he's a self-made real estate multi-millionaire – I know it will be a big success. The Lord wants His people to live abundantly.

I will miss you, but Indiana isn't that far away, and that's why the Lord made airplanes.

Your loving, loving mother,
'Paqu'

271

We had for a brief time a civilization that clung to a thin strip of land between the ocean and the desert.

Water was our problem, too much of it on one side, too little on the other, but it didn't stop us. We built houses, highways, hotels, shopping malls, condo complexes, parking lots, parking structures, schools, and stadiums.

We proclaimed the freedom of the individual, bought and drove millions of cars to prove it, built more roads for the cars to drive on so we could go the everywhere that was nowhere. We watered our lawns, we washed our cars, we gulped plastic bottles of water to stay hydrated in our dehydrated land, we put up water parks.

We built temples to our fantasies – film studios, amusement parks, crystal cathedrals, megachurches – and flocked to them.

We went to the beach, rode the waves, and poured our waste into the water we said we loved.

We reinvented ourselves every day, remade our culture, locked ourselves in gated communities, we ate healthy food, we gave up smoking, we lifted our faces while avoiding the sun, we had our skin peeled, our lines removed, our fat sucked away like our unwanted babies, we defied aging and death.

We made gods of wealth and health.

A religion of narcissism.

In the end, we worshipped only ourselves.

In the end, it wasn't enough.

272

A crossroads out in the desert.

Because why not?

There's a convenient pullover where the cars can pull up and make the trade.

And Elena's troops can gun them all down and

be gone long before the sheriffs or the INS can get there.

They all know this.

Lado knows it.

His men sure as hell know it.

Any reader of Western fiction or fan of Western movies knows it.

Ben and Chon know it.

And go anyway.

Because it has to happen.

273

They take the pony, of course.

Loaded with two shotguns, two pistols, and two AR-15s.

If they're going out, they're going out blazing.

Shoot Magdalena up with just enough junk to keep her docile and walk her out of her motel arm-in-arm-in-arm. Put her in the backseat, tape her mouth shut and her wrists in front of her.

Long quiet drive out to the desert.

What's there to talk about and what do you put on the radio as a soundtrack to kidnapping and killing?

Silence is better.

Nothing to say anyway.

274

For the first time in her life, Elena feels sheer terror.

A nausea deep in her stomach.

And the time just . . . will . . . not . . . pass.

She jumps at the knock on her bedroom door.

Lado's wife, Delores.

She's on the verge of tears and Elena is strangely touched by her simpatico.

'Elena,' she says. 'I know you have . . . so much . . . on your mind, but—'

Her voice quivers and then she starts to cry.

'My dear friend,' Elena says. 'Whatever is so wrong?'

She puts her arm around the woman's shoulder, leads her into the room, and shuts the door behind them.

Delores tells Elena all about her husband, what he did, what he's done.

275

Short ride for O.

She's out for most of it on Ambien.

Pharmaceutical duct tape.

Wakes up shivering in the cold desert night.

'We're close,' Lado says.

So close, he thinks, to winning it all.

His men left an hour early and are in position around the pull-off.

276

Delores sobs and sobs.

Elena understands but tires of it quickly.

She pats her hand one more time, sits her up, and says, 'You did the right thing. You did what any woman would, to protect her children.'

Men teach us how to treat them.

277

Ben and Chon find the pull-off by the junction.

They pull over and blink their lights twice.

An answering signal comes out of the darkness and then a black SUV comes forward and stops about ten yards in front of them.

Chon can smell a night ambush and he smells it now, along with the creosote bush and Indian tobacco, the soft desert scents even on this chill night.

'They here?' Ben asks.

'Oh yeah,' Chon says. 'Both sides.'

Doubtless they're lying in the brush next to the pull-off and on the other side of the road.

'The second you get O,' Chon repeats, 'hit the ground and stay flat.'

'Yup.'

'Ben?'

'Yeah?'

'It's been a ride.'

'Yes, it has.'

Ben tucks a pistol into the back of his belt, takes Magda, and leads her out of the car.

Chon reaches in back and grabs the two ARs.

Lado sticks a pistol in his own belt, walks around to the passenger side, and pulls O out of the car.

The little cunt is still out of it.

Her legs wobbly.

They should be, Lado thinks, after what I gave her.

He walks toward the *gueros'* car.

Elena gets out of the Land Rover. Hernan at her side.

She sees one of the bastards walking with Magda in front of him.

Thank God, thank God, thank God.

As soon as he releases her, the men know to open up.

'Let her go!' Lado shouts. 'Send her my way!'

'You, too!' Ben answers.

He gives Magda a gentle push toward Lado.

Lado does the same with O.

As soon as Magda is out of Ben's reach, Elena nods her head.

The night lights up.

Bright red muzzle flashes from twelve guns, all trained on

Lado.
As Elena shouts, '*Dido!*'
Informer.
What Delores told her.

281

Lado does a Wicked Witch of the West.
Melts in front of Dorothy O as
Ben rushes forward, tackles her, and presses her
to the ground and they watch
Lado dance a funny little jig
Light on his feet, as they say, for a big man,
he tiptoes back toward his car like he still
thinks he can get in and drive away from this,
but then he trips on himself and falls face-first
on the hood then slides down, his blood leaving
a smear on the shiny black paint.
A shooter comes out of the darkness, grabs him
by the hair, and jerks his neck back.
The machete is a silver flash in the moonlight.

282

Then it's quiet.
Save for Magda, screaming under her gag,
stumbling into her mother's arms.
Who says
'Kill them.'

283

The world erupts in fire.

Ben presses O deeper into the ground but she squirms out from under him and

Scrambles across the desert floor, grabs Lado's pistol from the ground, and starts to fire and so Ben

Starts shooting as

284

One rifle cradled in front of him, the other looped over his back, Chon belly-crawls toward Ben and O, shooting as he moves. He aims at each muzzle flash and the *sicarios* don't know enough to fire and move.

Flashback.

Night ambushes in the Stan but

He knows he's fighting now for Ben and O

They are

His country.

285

Suddenly it's quiet.

Cautiously, Chon gets up to see

Bathed in moonlight, Elena sits on the ground, her back against the grill of the Land Rover. Two dead *sicarios*, neatly shot through the forehead, lie beside her like sleeping guard dogs.

Elena calls, 'Magda! Magda!'

Chon sees the girl stumble in the greasewood and brush, trying to get away from the scene.

Thinks, there will be time for her later.

He points his rifle at Elena's head.

She looks up at him and says, 'Do it. You already killed my son.'

O is standing at his shoulder.

Blood – black in the silver light – runs down her tattooed arm like a jungle waterfall. It flows from the mermaid's mouth and winds down the undersea vines.

Chon tries to raise the gun but his wounded shoulder won't let him. His arm goes numb and the rifle falls into the dirt.

Says, 'I can't.'

Elena smiles at O. And says, 'You see, *m'ija?* You see what men are?'

O picks up Chon's fallen rifle.

Says, 'I'm not your fucking daughter.'

And pulls the trigger.

286

Chon catches up with Magda, in shock, stumbling around the desert, and grabs her wrist.

He knows what he needs to do, if they're to get away. They all know it – if they let this girl live, they run tonight and can never come home again.

Chon looks over.

O shakes her head.

Ben does the same.

Chon rips the tape off the girl's mouth, then her wrists. He shoves her toward the Suburban. 'Get the fuck out of here. Get the fuck out of here now.'

She staggers toward the car and gets in. A few seconds later the car rooster-tails out of the dirt and onto the highway.

Chon walks over to Ben and O.

Just as Ben

Collapses.

287

Chon kneels beside them, rolls Ben over as gently as he can but Ben screams in pain.

Opening Ben's jacket, Chon sees and knows.

Gets the morphine and the syringe from his own pocket.

He finds a vein in Ben's arm and shoots him up.

288

O asks,

'He's going to die anyway, isn't he?'

'Yes.'

'I don't want to leave him.'

'No.'

Chon breaks another ampoule and fills the syringe. O offers her arm. Chon finds a vein and shoots her up.

Then he repeats the process on himself.

322

289

O lies down and wraps her arms around Ben.
He presses his back against her warm stomach.
'You'd like Indo,' he mutters.
'I'll bet.'
O strokes his cheek. Warm, soft Ben. She says, 'Tell me about it.'

Dreamily, Ben tells her about golden beaches edged in emerald necklaces of jungle. About water so green and blue that only a stoned God could have dreamed up the colors. Tells her about crazy, motley birds doing Charlie Parker riffs at the incitement of sunrise, about small-framed brown men and delicate brown women with smiles as white and pure as winter and hearts to match. About sunsets of gentle fire, warm but not burning, satin black nights lit only by starshine.

'It sounds like heaven,' she says. Then, 'I'm cold.'

Chon lies down behind O and presses close. The warmth of his body feels good to her. He reaches his arm over her and takes Ben's hand.

Ben grips it hard.

290

O listens to the sounds in her head.
Waves gently breaking on pebbles.
She hears her heartbeat, and her men's.
Strong, but slowing.

Warm now in the womb of her two men.

O.

We'll live on the beach and eat the fish that we catch. We'll pick fresh fruit and climb trees for coconuts. We'll sleep together on palm frond mats and make love.

Like savages.

Beautiful, beautiful savages.